Losing it

Sandy McKay

Longacre Press

Acknowledgements:

Losing It was written with the assistance of
a Creative New Zealand New Work grant.

Several years ago, while researching for an article,
I advertised in the newspaper for people who were
willing to share their experience of anorexia and/or
bulimia. I am grateful to the women who replied and
who agreed to talk to me. Without their openness
and honesty this book would not have been written.
Special thanks also, to Emma Neale for her
encouragement and editing expertise.
And to Keri for his 'Fat Cat' poem.

First published with the assistance of

ARTS COUNCIL OF NEW ZEALAND *TOI AOTEAROA*

ISBN: 978 1 877361 74 6

A catalogue record for this book is available from
the National Library of New Zealand.

First published by Longacre Press, 2007
30 Moray Place, Dunedin, New Zealand.

Book and cover design by Christine Buess
Sketches on pages 61 and 118 by Katy Buess
Cover photograph by Lucinda King
Printed by Griffin Press, Australia

www.longacre.co.nz

There is a line in *Charlotte's Web* that says,
"It is not often that someone comes along who is a
true friend and a good writer."

This book is for all my writer friends – especially
Robyn Yousef, Gillian Thomas, Alex Fusco,
Susan Frame, Maclean Barker and 'Uncle Mac'.

And for Karyn, whose courage I so admire.

Dear Issy,

This place sucks. And that's sucks with a capital S. Honestly, Issy! This place is the pits.

The people are nutters, including the staff.

Do you remember that relieving maths teacher we had last year? The one who used to pick at his teeth gunge with Miss Pratchett's protractor? We called him Professor Plaque. Well, guess what? Professor Plaque has been reincarnated as a mental health specialist. Lucky me! I get to be interviewed (or should I say interrogated), by this guy on a regular basis. Talk about nosey. He practically wants to know when I had my last crap. Correction, he ACTUALLY wants to know when I had my last crap. Or bowel movement, as he calls it.

'Has there been a bowel movement in the last twenty-four hours, Johanna?' asks he.

'Mind your own business, Plaquey boy,' answer I. (Not really, but I'd like to.)

I'll go bonkers in here, Issy. It's like prison except worse because at least in prison you have some freedoms.

Like … even murderers can choose if they want dinner or not. Even rapists and child molesters and guys who don't pay income tax are allowed to say 'No thanks. I'll pass on the lumpy spuds and soggy silver beet, if you don't mind.' Not me. In here they're allowed to stuff anything down your neck because that's their job. Last night a nurse tried to con me into eating pasta. I mean, it's okay for her because she's fat already and she has a face like a reflection in a stainless steel teapot and she's coming at me with 217 calories per spoonful, and, well… I'm sweating at the sight of it. So, I panic and, um, well, it gets a tad messy… pasta goes everywhere.

But then she has the cheek to go off at ME, like it's all MY fault. Okay, so a teeny weeny bit might have landed on her jumper but I wasn't taking any chances. I'd have to do a million press ups to work off those calories. Either that or throw it up again.

Of course, that's not allowed either. Hell, no. All vomiting prohibited, by order of the hospital Gestapo. In here the nurses actually come to the bog with you. Like, how bad is that?! They stand outside waiting, listening at the door. Perverts!

It's hard to describe what this place is like.

It smells weird. Think Toilet Duck and boiled cabbage. Hmmmnnnnn…

It feels weird too. Like they don't trust you. Like you're a naughty little kid.

I feel like I've fallen down a hole. Like I'm in one of

those dreams where you're calling for help but your voice won't work and no one can hear you. HELP!

God, Issy, you're my only connection with the outside world. Please write back asap. Please swear on all that is precious to you (those new burgundy Doc Martens will do) that you will faithfully and honestly answer my letters.

Yesterday they told me I wasn't allowed visitors. But how can they do that?! Even prisoners are allowed visitors – unless they've done something really annoying, like starting a riot or something. Which might not be a bad idea, except that, well, just starting a conversation is hard enough right now…

Actually, it's a miracle I'm allowed to write this letter. It took some doing just getting the paper and God knows what they thought I was going to do with it. Make a paper chain to hang myself? Slash my wrists with a ballpoint pen? They even confiscated my razor on arrival. Did I tell you that? Imagine the state of my leg hair this time next week.

Professor Plaque Mark II has a ginger moustache and a little red tuft on his chin. Gross. He also talks real slow and makes these clicking noises in his throat when he's trying to decide about something important, like should this new girl be given paper to write to her best friend on.

It's all such a big deal, like they're trying to find the reason for everything you do. Well, they're not going to find my reason, because there isn't one. I'm a grown person, free to make my own decisions.

Well, I used to be. (Didn't I??)
Please write back soon, Issy,
Luv from,
Jo

XXXXXXX

Dear Jo,

Of course I'll write back. I will write to you whenever
I can … Okay?!

You are scaring me big time, Jo. It can't be that bad.
Can it? I didn't get any sleep last night for thinking about
you. In fact I tossed and turned so much that Pavlova
finished up on Meredith's bed and things have to be pretty
bad for Pav to sleep with Meredith. (Let's face it; things
have to be pretty bad for anyone to sleep with Meredith!)

Anyway, during my tossing and turning I remembered
this old movie Mum bought at the Video Ezy two-for-
the-price-of-one sale. *One Flew Over the Cuckoo's Nest* or
something. She thought it was a film about bird life but it
turned out to be about a guy who was put into a mental
hospital by mistake. The point is, this guy escaped in the
end. (Well, someone did.) Hang on to that thought, Jo.
Think positive.

So … what is your room like?

I got such a shock when your Dad told me you'd gone

into hospital. I didn't realise … I thought you were wagging. Well, I know how much you hate Science and we were doing all that boring electric current stuff and I know you were finding those circuit diagrams difficult and … Anyway, I thought you'd just bunked off. I couldn't believe it when your dad said … well … you know …

If it's any consolation, Mum says it's a good hospital you're in. Don't ask me how she knows that but you know what a know-all she is and how schoolteachers know absolutely everything. (Do you realise that sentence has four 'knows' in it? Lucky Mum's not reading this or she'd make me do a rewrite.)

She sends her love, by the way. Her advice is 'do what the doctor says and eat all your vegies'. Sorry if that isn't much help but I'm sure she means well. (Don't you hate it when people say that? She *means* well – just an excuse for poking your nose in if you ask me.)

Speaking of poking your nose in … Mum's been watching me like a hawk lately and I get second helpings of absolutely everything. Pathetic really. As if someone who can scoff down five sausage rolls and two jelly donuts (yesterday's lunch) will ever get anorexia. As you know I couldn't stick to a diet if my life depended on it.

I feel so helpless up here, Jo, but if writing helps then I'll write. We'll be penfriends.

Remember those penfriends from Wellington we had in Year Six? Mine was a boy called Robert who only ever wrote about soccer. Once he told me he'd scored an 'own goal' and I wrote back saying 'congratulations' and then he stopped writing. I could never figure that one out. I promise I won't write to you about soccer. Yours was Vicki somebody who did tap dancing and collected stamps and you sent her your dad's stamp collection. Remember? I think you got in trouble for that.

Well, I better go, Jo. Mum's nagging at me to set the table. We're having spaghetti bolognaise for dinner with spewey cheese, which is Dad's pet name for parmesan.

Be good and eat your vegies.

Lots of luv,

Issy

P.S. You'll be home again in no time. Trust me.

P.P.S. Wasn't it a compass Professor Plaque picked his teeth with? A protractor is the plastic semi-circle thing – difficult to fit inside a mouth!

P.P.P.S. And does anyone collect stamps any more? (Well, let's face it, apart from two obvious exceptions, does anyone send letters any more?)

Dear Issy,

Your letters are my life saver – please keep them coming.
Just the sight of your handwriting cheers me up heaps.
Yeah. I'd forgotten about Vicki. You're right; I was in a
power of trouble over that. Dad had been collecting those
stamps forever but I could hardly ask for them back, could
I? And you are probably right about the protractor too,
which explains why I'm so hopeless at maths.

Sorry if I went off a bit last time. After the pasta
episode they gave me some medication, which was supposed
to calm me down but seemed to do the opposite. In fact,
I hardly slept for two days with my brain buzzing like one
of Mr T.'s parallel circuits.

You asked about my room. Prepare to be bored. The
walls are the colour of porridge. There are some windows
along one side but not the kind that open. Only the very
high up ones open. I guess that's to discourage inmates
from escaping, which must be tempting at times. The
curtains are multi-coloured squiggles and probably
designed by a preschooler high on Coca Cola. On the wall
by my bed there's a painting of a lighthouse with waves
crashing around it. (The painting looks familiar; I've seen
it before somewhere.) Actually, the painting is the least
crappy thing in the room. Well, it's not snow-capped
mountains or tulips or fake apples in a bowl like they have
at the doctor's.

Moving right along … the bed is metal grey – no

duvet, just sheets and a white cotton bedspread – same as everyone else. Most of the time I am freezing cold. Oh, and there's a set of drawers too, for clothes and stuff. Not that I've brought much to wear...

I'm on the third floor and there's a garden down below. Some of the patients go there to smoke cigarettes. I don't think I'm allowed outside yet because even leaving the ward for a stroll is a privilege you get when you've put on weight.

See what I mean about being treated like a kid?

Must go now.

Luv,

Jo

P.S. Oh, yeah, I forgot. There's a locker in my room too, and a pot plant with leaf disease – my inheritance from the last inmate.

Dear Jo,

A quick run down on school news. In Science we've moved
on to 'helpful and harmful bacteria'. Tomorrow we're
going to grow some bacteria ourselves.

Today we learned how sneezes can travel at 300 kms
per hour. (I kid you not!) So you're not missing much!

Are you allowed to drink coffee in there? (Just a random
enquiry.)

Best wishes,

Issy

Dear Issy,

Hey! Fancy a sneeze moving that fast! The question is,
how do they measure it and why would anyone want to?

Yes, we are allowed to drink coffee. Don't get too
excited though, it's only instant. We have a 'common
room' here, which is just a weird word for lounge (it's
complete with a TV and bookshelves and stuff). We are
allowed coffee, tea or Milo. There is also a filtered water
unit and a jar full of stale gingernuts.

The furniture consists of three corduroy beanbags,
two tatty armchairs and a long leather couch covered with
a pukey green crocheted blanket. For added entertainment

we have state of the art games like Snakes and Ladders, Chinese Checkers and Trivial Pursuit. 'Ho hum, by gum' as Mr Tafea would say. There's a room off the side of the lounge that they use for group therapy sessions. I haven't been to one yet and can't say I'm looking forward to it. In fact, I'm dreading it. But the doc says I should be starting next week.

Oh, and there's a noticeboard in the common room. People put up all sorts of weird stuff – like poems and cards and that. Mostly I just make coffee and go back to my room.

Bacteria … hmmnnnn … fancy growing your own germs. Like, as if there aren't enough in this world already?!

Science sucks. I reckon English is the only subject worth doing at school – especially Shakespeare. (I know you can't stand the guy but I think he's awesome.) Remember when we did *Macbeth* in Year Ten and we saw it performed at the Playhouse? Remember the whole class trekking into town and cramming into that little theatre with those boys from St Paul's (all ponging of smelly feet and BO)? That play was so cool. Gemma Scott nearly wet her pants at the end when they brought Macbeth's head in on that pole. God, it looked real. I loved the witches best. 'Double, double, toil and trouble, fire burn and cauldron bubble –' and all that other stuff about newts and frogs, tongues and stuff. I wonder if we're doing Shakespeare this year. Maybe you'll study him while I'm in here.

Speaking of which, has anyone noticed my disappearance? Silly question – course they have. Mr Tafea won't
have anyone to pick on. I hope you made up some great
story like I've gone off with Mum on a world trip or
something. You could say she turned up unexpectedly,
demanding I accompany her on a Pacific island cruise to
celebrate. I could send a postcard to make it look real. Or
maybe you could say I won the ANZAC essay competition
and got flown direct to Gallipoli.

Doesn't matter what you tell them, Issy, so long as
it's not the truth. Promise you won't tell the truth about
where I am.

Luv,

Jo

Dear Jo,

Don't worry about what's going on at school. You just concentrate on getting well. Hey, I found out that someone
from Mum's school went to your hospital last year – for
bulimia (is that what they call the throwing up thing?).
Anyway, apparently, she's doing real well and still goes
down once a week as a day patient. Perhaps you could do
something like that. Hope so.

    Missing you heaps,

    Issy

P.S. The experiment with bacteria was actually quite interesting. (My God, you should see how fast it grows.) Except
that the swab taken from Donald Dingley's teeth would
put you off kissing forever. Ugghh!

Noticeboard:

LOST

Has anyone seen our game of Trivial Pursuit?
Please return to games cupboard. Several Chinese
Checkers are also missing.

Dear Issy,

Don't worry about me – I'm going to be fine.
Correction, I AM fine. I'm here under false pretences
and the more I see of this place the more I know I don't
belong. I don't have a problem, I'm not crazy and I don't
need help. In fact, if I hadn't given myself that mad
haircut I wouldn't even be here.

Some of the others are nutters, though. There's one
called Caroline, for example, who is completely off the
planet. She seems okay when you first meet her, but she's
really weird.

Example – she came into my room the other day
wanting laxatives. I've never taken laxatives but she
wouldn't believe me.

'You're lying,' she said. 'Everyone takes laxatives.'

So I said, well, no, actually they don't, but then she

19

started rummaging through my locker. Unbelievable. Like, here is this stranger unzipping my toilet bag. 'You must have some,' she said, getting all frantic and red in the face. Then she spied Paddy. (Remember the old teddy Mum gave me not long before she left?) Anyway, she started giving Paddy the once over, like a strip search on *Border Patrol* or something. He's too old to be manhandled like that so I grabbed him back. But then she thought I was hiding something and, well … I managed to convince her in the end but it took a while. See what I'm up against?

With love from your nuthouse friend,

Jo

P.S. You didn't answer my questions about school, which must mean they all know. Miss Hughes told everyone where I am, didn't she? Only, I thought school counsellors were like priests and lawyers and hair removal specialists – bound by oaths of secrecy. I'm a big girl, Issy. Please tell me the truth.

Dear Jo,

You are NOT a big girl, that's the whole point. Sorry I
didn't mention the school stuff. I just forgot and really,
it's no big deal. I couldn't tell that tale about you going
off with your mum on a cruise because Miss Haddock
beat me to it. She told the class you weren't well and were
spending time in hospital. That's all she said. Honest. And
when Gemma Scott and Zoe Barker came up at the end of
period to ask how you were I just played dumb and said
the doctors weren't sure but were putting it down to some
kind of mystery virus.

They were both sweetness and light. Gemma said she
thought you hadn't looked well for a while and Zoe even
asked if you were allowed visitors.

But don't panic, I said the doctors had you in quarantine to prevent cross-infection and I must have been
convincing because they both jumped back like I was
contagious or something. I guess all this bacteria stuff
has everyone worried and Donald Dingley's mouth swab
hasn't helped matters, either. Also, there's been heaps of
stuff in the paper about bird flu pandemics and the
teachers have even been showing us how to sneeze
properly. (To prevent the spread of germs you have to do
it in your elbow – sneeze, that is!)

Anyway, there's no need to worry because no one is
talking behind your back. I promise!

School is just as boring as ever. We are doing Pilates

for PE with Miss Rainer, which is kind of like yoga. We have these dinky little mats and do lots of focussing on our epicentre (whatever that is!!) and being aware of our breathing. (In, two, three, four – Out, two, three, four …) Trouble is, with Oliver Preston in the room, it's difficult to be aware of anything except his latest fart. There is something fermenting in that boy's gut, I'm sure of it.

For English we are doing transactional writing but don't ask me what that's about because I spent the whole period working on my maths homework.

Luv,

Issy

Dear Issy,

I think it's isolation, not quarantine. Isn't quarantine where Pavlova and Sushi will have to go when you and I do our OE? (Is that still a date, by the way?)

About Miss Hughes, I'd have to say I'm still not convinced, Issy. In fact, I reckon those school counsellors would spill the beans at the first sign of trouble. I bet they don't know the meaning of the word 'confidential'. Luckily, I didn't divulge all my worldly secrets. Maybe that's being paranoid but that's the way you get with this much time to think. The days all wobble into each other, like jelly.

Sometimes all I do is lie here looking at the curtains, which might not be quite so bad if they were decent curtains – these ones don't even meet in the middle. (Things like this take on great significance in a psychiatric ward.) The curtains dangle like limp dishcloths. Pull yourselves together, I tell them. Smarten yourselves up, for goodness' sake. But it doesn't make a scrap of difference.

The only interesting thing is that a spider is building a web in the corner. Which reminds me of the story *Charlotte's Web*, which Mum read to me when I was little. It was all about a spider called Charlotte and a pig called Wilbur and how the spider tried to save the pig's life by making it famous but in the end she died herself. Well, I think she died. We never made it to the end because we knew what was going to happen and neither of us wanted Charlotte to die – so we made up our own fake happy ending instead. We were good at that. Fake, happy. Happy, fake.

Anyway, just to be breathtakingly original, I've called this spider Charlotte.

Lots of love,
Jo

Dear Issy,

I haven't had a letter in days. God, I hope you're not getting sick of writing. Please tell me you're not getting sick of writing. I know my last letter was a bit manic and I shouldn't unload on you like that.

I've been told I have to start group therapy tomorrow, so I hope that'll help. I had a session with a different doctor yesterday who gave me this lecture about anorexia. She talked about it like it was cancer or something and if I didn't respond to treatment I'd die. Talk about dramatic and over the top! Talk about scare tactics!! She said if I didn't put on weight I'd be put on something called bed rest, which sounds like totally out of the Dark Ages.

Apparently, I've been diagnosed with both anorexia and bulimia. Lucky me. I didn't know you could have both at the same time. The staff here seem hell bent on tagging us all with something.

I looked up 'anorexia' in the Scrabble dictionary yesterday. It said 'absence of appetite or desire'. Well, so what? There must be worse things. I mean, what's so great about appetite and desire in the first place? And haven't these people got better things to do than muck about with the likes of me? Because really, when you think about it, there must be loads more interesting heads to read than mine. Like psychopaths and rapists, for example, and people who can't stop nicking stuff (like old Mrs Ramsay down the road who took to shoplifting after her husband died, even though he'd left her pots of dough). Those people need help more than I do. Since when was not eating against the law?

And what's the cure, anyway? Stuffing macaroni down our throats and banning physical activity? Oh yeah, I forgot to tell you. Exercise is a privilege in this place. Like going to the shop, having visitors, peeing in private and just about every other normal endeavour.

Have to go now.

Please write soon.

Your friend,
Jo

Dear Jo,

Lucky old you. Wish I didn't have to do exercise. Miss Rainer has just announced that from next week on we'll be in training for the school formal, which means learning all those stuffy old-fashioned dances. One – two – three – twirl... Ha! (Stomp – stomp – stomp – clunk... more like.) I think I can feel a doctor's appointment coming on.

    Luv,

    Issy

P.S. Please find enclosed this photograph of me and Pavlova. Sorry about the blurry bits – I used the self-timer. My technique obviously needs practice.

Dear Issy,

Thanks for the photograph. You and Pavlova now have pride of place on the cabinet, beside the long-suffering pot plant. This afternoon I had my first group counselling session. The doctor thought it'd be a good idea and I couldn't be bothered arguing. Not after last time. Besides, I am bored shitless on my own all day.

    Actually, I'm glad I went because it was good to meet the others properly. There were six of us today. According

to one of the nurse aides, most of us have some kind
of eating disorder. (I guess that includes me.) There are
other problems too, she says, but most are eating related.

I am definitely the fattest in the group.

The therapist's name is Veronica Brown. She looks
about the same age as your mum and quite pretty in an
arty farty kind of way. She wears interesting jewellery
– like curtain rings in her ears and a large turquoise snake
on her pinky. She doesn't say much but nods a lot and
sometimes she looks at you so hard that you wonder if
you've got a pimple on your nose or perhaps you haven't
washed your face properly or maybe there's a booger
dangling somewhere gross. A bit off-putting.

There's only one guy in the group. Leon. He has dark
floppy hair and green cat eyes like your Pavlova. There's
a girl called Tegan with bad skin and frizzy red hair.
And another called Ingrid, who has long blonde hair like
someone out of a shampoo ad except that she looks like
she's going to burst into tears all the time. Actually, she
has a Britney Spears look about her. There's also a girl
called Kara who's Asian. And then there's Caroline who
I already told you about. She seemed a bit more relaxed
today. Maybe her bowel movements are back on track.

Because it's my first time, everyone introduces themselves.

'Hi. My name's Tegan and I love horses. My favourite
horse is called Bianca but she died last year...'

'My name is Ingrid and I've been here six months...'

27

'Hi, I'm Kara–'

'I'm Leon, King of Trivial Pursuit.' (Is he for real?)

'Caroline.'

The session goes for about an hour. At first I am pretty nervous, hoping I'm not expected to tell my life story to six strangers. They'd die of boredom anyway.

We all sit in a half circle. As it turns out most of the session focuses on Kara's hand washing techniques. Yes, Issy, hand washing. The poor girl has some issue related to the washing of hands. It's called an obsessive-compulsive disorder. Leon told me, afterwards.

Anyway, her problem is that she gets hysterical about germs and is obsessed with everything being clean and perfect. Her room is absolutely mega tidy and she has a thing about not liking uneven numbers. She even had to change rooms when she arrived because they'd put her in room seven. And there's other stuff too, like Leon says she won't touch money that hasn't been soaked overnight in Janola. (Maybe she did NCEA Level 1 Science at school and freaked out.)

Leon is proving to be a mine of information once he gets going. He says Tegan is okay in small doses and Caroline is nutty as a fruitcake but not too bad when you get to know her.

Ingrid sounds the most interesting. Apparently she is a talented runner who made the New Zealand Athletics team. But then she started training too hard and not eating right and the coach got worried and refused to continue coaching until she'd put on weight. That was almost a year ago and she missed out on getting picked for the Commonwealth Games and got really depressed. The coach visits her quite a lot. According to Leon he's an old guy, in his sixties, who still runs a million miles a week himself and looks like Mahatma Gandhi. Remember we did him last year for Social Studies? He used to wear that loincloth and go on fasts all the time. (So how come he stops eating and becomes a hero while I get banged up in here?) Leon doesn't say much about himself except to warn me that if I hear strange sounds coming from room 19, not to worry because that'll be him practising guitar. He's teaching himself from the Internet and although he really likes Ben Harper (he's got the *Diamonds on the Inside* CD) his favourite musician of all time is actually Bob Dylan. This week he's learning 'Blowing in the Wind'.

Letter 2

Have just realised that I forgot to post my first letter so I'll post them both together. It's now Wednesday and I'm relieved to report that I survived another group session. Far out, Issy. Group therapy is so not me. You know how I hate all that touchy feely stuff. Well, that's what group's like. We sit in a circle (because it's less threatening, according to the therapist) and we're supposed to 'share' stuff – like feelings and problems and that.

So, it's pretty hard going most of the time and there are truckloads of silences. Veronica usually tries to get the ball rolling. She'll say something lame about some problem she has at home. Like, today she told us about this argument she had with her partner over the remote control on the TV set. Then she asked how we felt about our own remote controls at home. No kidding, Issy. Your relationship with your remote control may be more revealing than you think!

At first I wondered if she was having us on but no, she was totally serious, and then I figured that discussing my feelings about remote controls couldn't hurt too much so I said, 'I don't really care who has the remote because, apart from *Shortland Street*, I don't watch much tele.'

'Thank you for sharing that with us, Johanna,' she said, as if I'd just revealed my most intimate secret. Leon was next. He said he was the only one in his house who watched TV because his mum was never home and his dad moved out last year. He watches *Shortland Street* too. (Had a good conversation about Hugo the other day.)

Then it was Kara's turn. 'I think remote controls are breeding grounds for germs and should be disinfected daily!' Hmmmnnnn… I see what Leon means.

I can't remember what Ingrid's contribution was but Tegan said something like she had no time for TV because she was always outside with the horse. Weird, huh. Once she gets onto the horse subject, there's no stopping her. She reminds me of Heather White back in Year Seven, who wouldn't read a book unless it had a horse on the cover. (Remember? She wore her hair in plaits and had two apples a day for play lunch.) Anyhow, Veronica finally managed to get a word in and we moved onto a new topic.

Today it was goals. You know, like things to aim for – (not as in soccer!)

I must confess, Issy, I quite like goals. So I put up my hand and said, um, yes, I did have a goal. Then Veronica said would I like to share it with the group. So I said my goal was to lose three kilos. Dumb, I know, because obviously you're not supposed to say stuff like that in here and Veronica flashed me this look, which translated into 'Let's try and think of something more sensible, shall we?'

So then I said the next thing that came into my head, which was something to the effect that I wanted to beat Leon at Trivial Pursuit. Where that came from I have no idea. But now I've opened my big gob and I haven't a hope in hell of beating Leon because he's like this absolute general knowledge freak and I know bugger all. Any suggestions?

Write back soon,

Jo

P.S. Practice Trivial Pursuit Questions:
How much Monopoly money do you collect for finishing second in a beauty contest?
Who's the orphan in The Adventures of Tom Sawyer – *Huck Finn, Tom Sawyer or Betty Thatcher?*

What country is Tobruk in?

P.P.S. Do you have anything interesting you could send me to read? All they have here are some ancient *Woman's Weekly*s and two *National Geographic*s. (Good photos but not much of a plot.)

Dear Jo,

'Whatever the challenge, whatever the test, whatever you're striving for, give it your best.' That's Miss Haddock's latest school motto.

P.S. Sorry, can't help on the general knowledge front.

P.P.S. I'll see what I can do about books.

Dear Issy,

The answers are – $10, Tom Sawyer, and Libya.

I'm slowly getting to know the staff here. There's a Samoan nurse called Bruce who whistles all the time and another woman called Morag who has such a strong Scottish accent that I can't understand a word she says. Leon calls her 'mean old Morag', which kind of suits. I like the nurse aides best. They're more down to earth. My favourite is Dot. Remember how I told you about the accident with the pasta? Well, that's her. She doesn't seem to hold that against me though, which is a relief.

And then there are the counsellors! Veronica is the one we have most often. Some of our discussions get pretty weird. They must have a laugh thinking up stuff. Like, yesterday Veronica had a copy of *Dolly* magazine and there was a photo of some girl in a bikini. The title of the article is 'I Think I'm Fat, Do You?' and what you think is supposed to reveal stuff about your personality.

Hmmnnnn…

Of course, it's obvious that the girl in the photograph IS fat and shouldn't wear a bikini but you're not supposed to think that because you're supposed to think there's nothing wrong with being fat. It's part of the therapy. Like, if they convince us there's nothing wrong with being fat we will all turn into dumplings and roly-poly happily home. Fat chance!

Anyway, Veronica uses the bikini girl as a discussion topic.

And the discussion goes like this.

Tegan first. 'That girl looks just like Amanda from pony club and she –' Blah, blah, blah completely off the subject…

Then it's Caroline, who studies the photograph for a moment before saying exactly what the rest of us think. Namely, that the girl has two chins, no waist, poxy thighs and would be miles better off in a kaftan than a bikini.

Ingrid (who is one of life's genuine sweet people) says good luck to her and people should be able to wear whatever they like. Kara says nothing, just sits there, picking some imaginary fluff off her jumper and being careful not to touch the pages of the magazine in case of contamination.

When it comes to Leon he just rolls his eyes and says personally the woman in the photograph doesn't do anything for him, bikini or no bikini. Then Veronica says that personal attraction isn't the object of the exercise here, Leon, and poor Leon goes bright red.

Interesting.

My guess is that Leon's probably gay. (He's definitely got the voice for it.)

Anyway, then we get onto an article about friendship, which sparks off a miserable discussion because no one seems to have a friendship worth talking about. Except for me, of course.

Do you realise, Issy, that we've known each other almost half our lives? And in all that time we've only had one argument (well, one bad one), which we both promised never to mention again. I think that must be some kind of record.

And to celebrate I have written a poem. Well, actually, it's more of a work in progress because as you can see, there are still a few gaps.

Luv from,

Jo

P.S.

Ode to my Best Friend

She's always there to lend me gear
And tell me what to wear
If my hair's not great
She tells me straight
We're such a crazy pair.
Though I bore her with my letters
She's one of life's go-getters
                    Still working on this line!!
She picks me up when I am sad or when
        I'm feeling down
She never blabs or gets too mad or
        runs me out of town. (Nah, maybe not!)

A bit corny, I know, but I've been feeling a bit corny lately. Must be this place.

P.P.S. Veronica has this thing about writing. She reckons it's therapeutic. So … well, the thing is, I've decided to have a go at writing to Mum.

Dear Missing Persons Department,

I am trying to track down a person by the name of Miranda Morrison. She was last seen six and a half years ago wearing blue pyjamas with yellow ducks on them and driving a white car. My brother Matt was only four when she left and I was nine. Anyway, now I'm fifteen and I would really like to get in touch again and would appreciate your assistance.

    Yours sincerely,

    Johanna Morrison

Dear Miranda,
I am writing to

Dear Mandy,
Remember me?

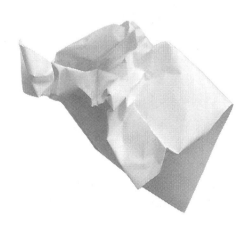

Dear Mum,

How are you these days? I know we haven't seen each other in a while but I've been thinking about you loads. I thought you might like to know how I'm doing. Actually, things aren't so hot at the moment. Nothing I can't deal with.

Well, to be honest,

Dearest Mother,
I am writing from the local nutfarm.

Dear Mum,

Well here I am at a camp for gifted and talented students.

We are here to get special help because the education system has been failing us. There's been stuff in the paper about it lately, you may have noticed. 'Special needs' works both ways these days and sometimes it's just as hard being bright as being thick.

Anyway, I know we haven't seen each other in a while but I thought you might like to know what's been happening in my life over the past few years. (More on that later.)

We are doing general knowledge at the moment. We have to know the answers to really difficult questions like: What does U.S.S.R. stand for? And what New Zealand scientist was one of the fathers of nuclear physics?

(Union of Soviet Socialist Republics and Ernest Rutherford, in case you were wondering.)

It was Dad's idea for me to come here. To tell the truth I reckon he just wanted some time out. He gets pretty stressed these days. (Probably comes from living with his 'gifted and talented' offspring!)

Actually, I bet he and Matt prefer it when I'm not around. It'll be just like flatting with no female in the house (apart from our cat, Sushi, that is). Matt is pretty cute for a brother. I mean, he can be annoying sometimes but overall he's pretty cool. We get along mostly. His one annoying thing is creepy crawlies. He's always finding little insects and stuff and putting them in jars with holes in the lid, where they usually end up dying of suffocation. His latest craze is worms. He tried to make a worm farm the other day by digging some worms out of the garden and putting them in a shoebox with his plastic farm toys. Cute, huh?

Anyway, you can't go anywhere without him finding something to bring home – like some old sheep bone, or a piece of driftwood, or a smelly old mussel shell that ends up stinking out his bedroom. Perhaps he should be an archaeologist when he grows up.

I have no idea what I should be. Sometimes I think just growing up will be a mission. One thing I'd like to do is travel. My best friend Issy and I fancy backpacking. Whenever we go past a backpacking place we say 'that'll be us one day' (with dreadlocks and Jesus sandals!). Then, after we're done with backpacking we'll probably get barmaiding jobs in London, meet famous rock stars and live happily ever after. Either that or come back here and be hairdressers. No, actually, scrap the hairdressing (I've done my dash with that for now) – Issy can be a scientist and I can be a famous writer.

Neither of us wants to get married and have kids, that's for sure. Bor-ing!

It's very quiet at this camp. A bit slack actually, because I'm not allowed visitors yet, which makes it difficult and sometimes lonely. Some of the others are a bit strange but I guess that's what happens when you're gifted and talented.

Anyway, I've prattled on enough.

I hope you are well.

Love from,
Your daughter Jo

Noticeboard:

> **Learn meditation.**
>
> Iyengar Yoga classes available on CD.

> **Feeling Angry?**
> 1. Admit your feelings.
> 2. Work out WHY you are angry.
> 3. Find some form of immediate release
>   (exercise, pillow bashing etc.).
> 4. Express your feelings to a trusted friend.
> 5. If something needs to be said, say it!

Dear Mum,

I've been in this place for nearly two weeks and it's hard work. It's not easy being gifted and talented. In fact, some might see it as a handicap. We do a lot of group work. Our ~~therapist~~ teacher likes to give us things to work on. She's into stuff like positive thinking and having goals and taking things one day at a time. Her favourite saying is 'Even the longest journey begins with the smallest step'. Pretty obvious when you think about it. Her other favourite saying is something to do with weeds just being flowers in the wrong place. I think she must be into gardening.

Some of the kids have had pretty interesting lives, which is probably why they've ended up here. There's a guy called Leon who is really nice. He's into 'old school' music. Bob Dylan is his all-time favourite. I told him we used to have his *Greatest Hits*. There's a stack of vinyl records in the cupboard at home but we don't have a turntable any more. Dad used to play this song by James Taylor, called 'Fire and Rain'. And there was another one called 'Time in a Bottle'. What a sad voice that guy's got. (James Taylor, I mean.) I quite like him as well.

We still have some of your gear at home, like clothes and that. Once I found a box of sewing stuff with patterns and fabric. Unfortunately I'm not that good at sewing. I made a skirt when I was in Year Eight but I put the zip in upside down and the waistband inside out. My friend

Issy's mum (who has just recently been promoted to school principal) had to fix it up.

Ingrid, Tegan, Kara, Caroline and Leon are the people in my group.

You'd like Ingrid. She looks like Britney Spears. And she's a runner. In fact, she might be going to the Commonwealth Games if she gets selected. She has her own coach and everything. Tegan is horse mad and never stops yakking.

We all get on pretty well, most of the time.

Your daughter,

Jo

Dear Issy,

These are the suckarse rules.

If you weigh less than 43 kilograms you are allowed to do bugger all. You're not allowed visitors. You're not allowed in the common room. You are not even allowed to wash your hair – so you lie here feeling (and smelling) like stink. And no one is allowed to talk to you, not even the nurses!

You are not supposed to write letters either, which is why this is not actually a real letter but just a figment of your imagination.

My Contract

This contract has been designed to help me stop vomiting, maintain my potassium levels and reach a discharge weight of 50 kilograms.

Currently I am vomiting several times a day. My potassiums level are low and I weigh 42 kilograms.

I agree to be on special unit until I reach a goal weight of 45 kilograms. A nurse will be with me during this time. This nurse may talk to me, help me with my records/contracted activities etc., but nothing else that can be considered a privilege. I realise this is in my best interest.

I agree to be on total bed rest (bed baths and bedpans, no walks) until my weight increases. I will work towards the privilege of being allowed off my bed. While I am on bed rest I can listen to my radio, read books and magazines, talk to a special nurse and complete records. I understand that bed rest will enable me to conserve energy and restore some body weight as well as controlling my vomiting behaviour. I understand it is for my own good.

For every twenty-four hours that I don't vomit I will do a negotiated activity: e.g. Watch Shortland Street, *make a phone call, write a letter, etc.*

Signed,

Johanna Morrison

Dear Jo,

Thanks for that poem. I especially loved the line about being 'one of life's go-getters'. Very inspirational. I have never thought of myself like that before and am tempted to show it to Meredith who is more convinced I'm one of life's couch potatoes. I know you probably only put it in to rhyme with 'letters' but it was a nice idea.

I have been thinking about writing a poem for you but I'm not that good at poetry. I could give it a try though...

Dear Issy,

One bad poet in the friendship is enough, Issy.
Hey, guess what? I did it. I started writing to Mum.

Dear Jo,

Wow! Jo. Your mum? Really?!

Hey, it must feel pretty strange after all these years. Well … I don't know how I'd feel … if my mum walked out like that. I don't know if …

Anyway, speaking of mothers, mine has gone up to Christchurch for a school principals' conference. Can you imagine it? A hotel full of bossy boots, all telling each other what to do! Of course, she's left us her usual seventeen-page instruction manual on how to survive without her.

I'm sure she wasn't that bad before she got the principal's job. Was she? She forgets we are all grown-ups now. I mean Dad's been a grown-up ever since she's known him (I bet he even popped out of Nan's tummy with an Adam's apple and a bald patch) and Kate is seventeen this year and Meredith is coming up twenty in September!!

Most girls are flatting at her age. And she would be too if she wasn't responsible for half the country's student debt. Trust her to go in for dentistry, which is about the most expensive thing you can study. So it looks like she'll be around the house for ages yet, which is a pity because it would be nice with just Kate and me for a change. (Kate is a lot more easygoing and not on my back all the time.) Siblingwise, three is not a good number and I reckon people should only be allowed to procreate in multiples of two. Kate and I are fine until Meredith comes home and then she and Kate take sides and I end up feeling on the outer.

Meredith has recently become a fitness freak and just because she spends half her life pounding a treadmill she thinks I should do the same. I told her I don't need to get on some boring treadmill when I've got tennis and she just snorts at me. And I say, what's wrong with playing tennis and she says, well, nothing, if you actually make an effort to run after the ball. So I say, hey, just because I don't stress about everything doesn't mean I don't enjoy it. And she says, but that's the problem, Issy, you'll never get anywhere in life by trying to enjoy things. Does that make any sense to you, Jo? Because it makes none to me at all. (She is so uptight, that girl, and God knows what she'll be like as a dentist. I pity her poor victims, er, I mean patients!)

School news. Hmmnnn ... there's an inter-school coming up next month and I'm supposed to be in the tennis team but Mariah Peters is challenging me for the number four spot so I might not make it. Actually, I am thinking about defaulting because it won't be any fun without you anyway. But don't tell Meredith or I'll never hear the end of it. (Silly me, trying to enjoy myself again.)

Oh, and guess what else. How could I forget? The most important thing: the date for the Senior Formal was announced in assembly. So you have to get yourself home by April 26 because you absolutely can't miss the formal. No way.

Anyway ... better get this posted. I'm making pancakes for dinner (not a vegetable in sight!). Also, I've got a book

46

review due in tomorrow and I haven't made it past chapter three yet.

Sometimes I wish I were in there with you, Jo. It must be like a vacation, with no homework to do or meals to cook. No parents breathing down your neck and laying down the law either. Make the most of it.

Luv,

Issy

P.S. How's the weight going? How much have you put on so far?

P.P.S. You'd have laughed in Science today. We've started on genetics. Mr T. says 'Can anyone explain the concept of sex determination?' So Danny Snell puts up his hand and says 'Is that like when someone's real determined to have sex, Sir?' Ha ha. Everyone cracks up.

Then, later on, Mr T. is doing a chromosome diagram and we have to work out if this cell is male or genetically abnormal. So Rebecca Short calls out, 'Do you think there's any difference, Sir?'

Even Mr T. had to laugh, though I could tell by the way he kept his back to us that he was trying really hard not to.

Dear Issy,

Yeah. Ha ha. Good one. And three cheers for Rebecca Short.

Shit, I'd forgotten about the school formal. Sometimes I feel like I'm in a glass bubble floating about in a fog.

Yesterday I spent most of the day in my room watching Charlotte trap a wasp. That was the sum total of my activity. (Unlike Charlotte who has so knackered herself that I haven't seen her move since.)

I found an article in the *National Geographic* about spiders, which I have pinned on my wall. Not exactly Robbie Williams but at least it covers a few cracks and gives me something to read. Like a project, kind of. I have now identified Charlotte as a brown spider. I must say I'm quite glad to have a roommate. I don't know if the cleaner's so fussed though. She nearly freaked out when she saw the photographs and she obviously hasn't spotted the real spider yet, which proves what a slackarse cleaner she must be.

Luv,

Jo

P.S. You must think I've gone nuts talking about a spider like that. Well, join the club!

Noticeboard:

> *'Let me be weightless and empty and light, then maybe I'll find peace tonight.'* F.C.

Dear Issy,

Good news. The doctor says I am allowed a visitor. Can you come this Saturday? Visiting hours are two till eight. Would your dad drive you, do you think? Oh, and, can you please bring some laxatives? Sorry, but I promised Caroline I'd ask. She says you should tell the chemist that you're really bunged up and need something strong. (The ones with senna work best, apparently.)

    Can't wait to see you again,

    Luv,

    Jo

Dear Jo,

Great news that you're allowed visitors. Does that mean
you've put on weight? Are you sure it's me you want to see
because if you're only allowed one visitor wouldn't it be
better to have your dad? Which reminds me …

The other day Kate and I bumped into your dad in the
supermarket. (We were stocking up on junk food for when
Mum's away.) Your dad had a trolley full of baked beans
and Jellimeat and was heading down the potato chip
aisle. Anyway, he didn't look good, Jo. In fact, he looked
pretty bad. He says you won't see him or even answer his
letters. I didn't tell him you were allowed a visitor because
he obviously didn't know. He is really worried about you,
Jo.

Luv,

Issy

P.S. Also, I bombed out with the laxatives. The chemist
shop man seemed awfully suspicious when I asked for
them and he insisted on selling me fifty grams of dried
prunes instead. Should I bring those?

Hi Jo,

It's Dad. How's it going?

Cracker weather lately. There's even been some talk of a drought. I'm not surprised because touch rugby's only been cancelled once all season, which has to be some kind of record — especially after last year.

Matt and I miss you heaps, Jo. The doctor says you're still pretty crook. I'd love to come and visit but if you don't want to see me then we'll have to make do with letters. Matt says he'll write when he gets around to it. You know what it's like trying to get that boy to sit still. Mrs Jordan reckons he's got ants in his pants. He had the school sports last week and Mr Campbell gave me the afternoon off so I could go watch. Not a bad wee hurdler, your brother, and he did quite well in long jump too.

Must take after his big sister, huh.

Mrs Jordan sends her love. She came over with a batch of shortbread last night. I told her there was no need but she seems to like a worthy cause. Oh well, better get off to bed. I'll have to let the cat out first. Which reminds me, Sushi is fretting big time and she's gone right off her Jelli-meat since you left.

Be good, Jo.
Lots of love,
Dad

Dear Issy,

Thank you so, so, so, so much for coming on Saturday. It was great to see you and good for you to see what this place is like. What did you think? It's not too bad, I guess, although the décor could do with a bit of a make-over. I know it's hard trying to talk in the lounge with everyone listening, which is probably why you were so quiet. What did you think of Leon? Did you notice his amazing green eyes?

Anyway, it bucked me up no end having you here and I felt almost human again by the time you left. I can't believe I didn't take you down to my room. You should have asked. I could have introduced you to Charlotte. Sorry, I'm just not thinking straight these days.

I hope your dad didn't mind coming all that way.

Luv,

Jo

P.S. Thanks for the prunes.

Advertisement on chemist shop window:

Dear Jo,

It was great seeing you on Saturday, too. I'm sorry I was
so quiet. To be honest, Jo, it was more of a shock than I
realised. I had no idea how thin you'd got. I feel so bad.
And guilty. You must have been like that before you went
into hospital. So how could I not have noticed?!! My best
friend turns into a skeleton right under my nose. I knew
you'd lost weight, but … well, you were always wearing
that baggy black top and …

I tried not to look shocked but when we hugged it
was … well, far out … You kept saying how quiet I was.
Mainly, I just wanted to cry. But I couldn't because … well,
how could I?

What kind of a friend must I be?

I shouldn't be going on like this, either. I should be supporting you, being positive and all that. But I'm worried, Jo. What are you doing to yourself? You've got to eat. Please...

Missing you heaps.

Your best friend forever,

Issy

Dear Mum,

There's not much happening here lately. We do a lot of talking but that's about it.

It's the outdoor education that I like best. I think we're getting onto that next week. I'm looking forward to kayaking and maybe abseiling, although I'm a bit scared of heights.

What is it you do again? Something to do with computers, was it? We could do with a computer in this place. You'd think the 'gifted and talented' would be first in line for technology. My friend, Leon has a laptop he uses for music. If we had a computer we could email each other. Send photos even. I'm dying to know what you look like now. It's been such a long time.

Dad told me once that you wanted to be a clothing designer and have your own label. Maybe you went off to do that. Hey Mum, do you remember a book called *Charlotte's Web*? You read it to me when I was little. It was about a spider and a pig but the ending got sad so we stopped reading. We pretended that Charlotte didn't die – do you remember? The pig's name was Wilbur and there was a rat called Templeton and the girl's name was Fern and there was someone else called Lurvy (weird name!), I think. The spider tries to save the pig's life and she does but … Yeah, well, anyway … I have a Charlotte in my room here. She's spinning her web as we speak. Yesterday she caught a big fat wasp. She's very clever. And she lives all on her own, without needing anyone at all.

Luv,

Jo

Toilet graffiti:

They said, smile and be happy, things could be worse.
So I smiled and was happy and things did get worse.

Yeah, know the feeling!

Noticeboard:

Patients' rights

You have the right to privacy and the right
to fair and proper treatment.
Your rights are outlined clearly under the mental health act.
A copy of this document is available on request.

Develop Inner Strength

- Speak your truth even if others find this difficult.
- Be courageous and move forward, even if this feels uncomfortable.
- Don't compare yourself with others.
- Take full responsibility for your actions.
- Show compassion.
- Step out of your comfort zone.
- Always face facts – denial leads to pain.

> Welcome to your new OT – Linley Clearwater
> will be taking a session here on Wednesday
> afternoon 1–3 p.m.
> This week you can learn how to make novelty
> chocolate. All those interested please meet in
> the common room at 1 p.m.

Toilet graffiti:

Do you ever feel alone and hopeless – like your soul is dead and you're a walking zombie?

Mmmnnnn ... sometimes.

'*All I need is the air that I breathe ...*' The Hollies
(an old school band from way back).

A poem by F.C.

My Secret Weapon

My secret weapon makes
me strong.
And wipes away
my tears.
My secret weapon numbs
my pain.
And casts aside
my fears.
My secret weapon protects
me well.
And makes me feel
invincibell.

Another poem by F.C.

The Shape of Things

Whittle me down
As far as you can
Carve my angles tight
A work of art, a body part
Chiselled cheekbones,
Nice and thin
Wrists like twigs
Shape and trim.

Dear Jo,

School is driving me nuts. Only five weeks to go and the whole of Cameron College is heading into 'formal' paranoia. Gemma and Zoe and Ruby Wheeler are positively ga-ga about their new outfits. Well, their impending new outfits. Apparently, Zoe's dad is taking them up to Christchurch in the weekend in his new Subaru station wagon (which Zoe just can't stop skiting about). I'm sure there are shops down here that sell posh frocks but they seem to think the ones in Christchurch will be posher.

In English, Miss Haddock got so sick of them wittering on that she split them up, which made it worse for me because now I'm in between Zoe and Gemma. Yesterday I was smack bang in the middle of this conversation about how Gemma's going to take all the hairs off forever with some wax strips she got at K-Mart.

Gemma – All you do is put a strip over the hair and then pull it off really fast so the hair comes out at the roots...

Zoe – Does it hurt?

Gemma – Don't think so.

Zoe – Can you do it, you know, down below, as well? (Giggle, giggle.)

Gemma – Don't see why not.

(Ow! Sounds painful to me!!)

Anyway, the big news for us is – drum roll, please... I've put both our names down for blind dates. Don't look at me like that, Jo. It'll be fun. I promise. There're some guys coming from St Paul's and you had to have your name in by Tuesday. I know we said we'd never do blind dates but I'm not taking any chances. Sometimes a girl's gotta face facts and the facts are that no one from Cameron College is going to ask me to the school formal. Clarke Ross was my one big hope but only because his mum is my mum's best friend. Anyway, his mum told my mum last week that he'd asked some girl called Sophie from the chess club. I was quite relieved actually because Clarke Ross is not exactly the most exciting guy on the planet. I think Mum was a bit disappointed though. ('Lovely boy, that Clarke. Lovely boy.') A blind date sounds like much more fun. Anyway, it's done now, so the next thing is to start thinking about outfits. Given that no one has offered to whisk us up to Christchurch we may have to settle for Mum's sewing machine. She says if we get the material organised by next week she might get them made in time. So, I went to Fabric Vision yesterday after school and I've sussed out a couple of patterns. I also managed to con the sales lady into cutting a few samples of fabric, which I have enclosed in this letter.

What do you think? The material will cost about thirty dollars a metre and we'll need about three and a half metres each. I was thinking maybe the purple for me and the aqua for you. The aqua would look stunning with your blonde hair.

Let me know as soon as you can because we don't have

much time. I'll need your measurements too. If you like the fabric then perhaps I should phone your dad and ask for some money. What do you think?

Luv,

Issy

P.S. This is a rough sketch of the outfits.

Dear Issy,

A blind date? Are you for real? We always said we'd never get blind dates. You could land up with anything. You could get some creepo with five chins and body odour. Or a psycho with two left feet! What if he's totally disgusting? What if he picks his nose? Or puts his tongue down your throat?

Count me out.

Jo,

What do you mean count you out? I can't. WE can't. Our names are down already. Do you really want to be the only sad-arse girl in the whole of Year Eleven who doesn't go to the formal? Can you imagine what it'd be like hearing it all second hand from the likes of Gemma and Zoe and Ruby Wheeler?

Issy

P.S. I am not taking 'no' for an answer. If you don't promise to come with me then I'm not writing you another letter.

Sorry, Issy, but I'm not in the mood for getting dolled up and going to a poxy dance with a total stranger. And have you really thought this thing through properly? Like, do we ask the blind date to come past the looney bin for a pick up? Huh? That'll be a turn on, won't it? (Sorry, but would you mind opening the door for me, please – strait-jackets are just so restricting these days!!)

Jo

Dear Jo,

Stop it! It's not funny you're in hospital and don't say stuff like that. It's not a looney bin.

Also, this is not some poxy dance! This is the Cameron College Senior Formal and I'm not going without you. Got that?! So make sure you're out by then. There are still five weeks to go, which is exactly thirty-five sleeps!!! I figure that two steak and cheese pies per day should just about nail it. Do it for me, Jo. Please. Pretty please. Pretty please with bells on.

Luv,
Issy

P.S. Please find enclosed one packet of Smarties to get you started.

P.P.S. The steak and cheese pie wouldn't fit in the envelope so I had to eat it myself!
P.P.P.S. Pull your head in, Johanna Morrison!

Dear Issy,

Thanks for the Smarties. I have eaten two blue ones already.

Sorry. You caught me on a bad day. I am a sarcastic cow and totally ungrateful. I don't deserve such a wonderful friend and I don't know why you put up with me. I promise to pull my head in from now on. (See? This is me, pulling my head in!) Anyway, the aqua is gorgeous and I think the purple would be awesome on you. I also thought your sleeve design was really inspired. What a good idea putting bells on the sleeves. Did you make that up yourself? Maybe you should think about becoming a clothes designer one day. I think the best thing would be to get yours made first and then I could try it on for size. I don't want to ask Dad for money.

Sorry if I sound a bit shitty but I've had a crap day.

It started with group therapy. Veronica is always trying so, so hard but it feels like we're going over the same old ground and not getting anywhere. You know, like in that movie *Groundhog Day*, where the guy gets stuck living the same day over and over and over.

Anyway, Tegan is really getting on my nerves and if I hear one more sob story about a dead horse, I'll scream. But you have to sit and listen and even if you've heard the story a million times you're not allowed to interrupt because it's against the rules. Even when Tegan's story is totally pathetic like it was today.

Aaaarrrgggghhhh!!! That's me screaming out the window in frustration!!

Kara is no better. Today she spent the entire session counting the tassels on a cushion. I can see her counting because her mouth is going like – one, two, three, four... and it drives me nuts. Then there's Ingrid – who is so pretty and talented and cute. What a waste! If she went to Cameron College she would be part of the in-crowd for sure, and she would have been asked to the formal a hundred times over. Instead she's in here. Well, anyway, it really got to me today, Issy – I felt so sad about everyone.

Even Caroline, who's not sad like Ingrid but has a hardness about her. She's all bitter and twisted up inside. I mean, she must be in her twenties and she's going nowhere. Well, I guess none of us are. It's like we've all come to the same dreary dead end.

Leon doesn't like Caroline much. His face closes over when she talks as if he's trying to ignore her. I'm not sure what that's about. So, it wasn't a good session. And to make things worse Veronica is on a feelings rampage again. 'How do you fe-e-e-e-l about that?' she says, giving us her sucky therapist look. Futile! Hopeless! Pissed off!

Fat! How the heck does she think we feel?! And who gives a toss, because it's feelings that got me into this mess to start with. Whoops! Wrong thing to say, because now Veronica pounces like a cat.

'What kind of feelings, Jo?' Don't you hate it when people go all neurotic and mushy about their fe-e-elings? I mean, it's not like you can die from hurt feelings. There are people in the world with not enough to eat and there are bombs going off and Aids is running rampant and Osama what's-his-handle is ready to blow us all to smithereens. What's the point in analysing every little feeling and going ga-ga over it?

I'm unloading again, Issy. Sorry. I'll shut up now.

Luv always,
Jo

P.S. *What country has the largest sheep population?*
(Australia)
Who was the first black man to win an Oscar?
(Sydney Poitier)
What is the most used word in written English?
(The)
What is observed the second Sunday in May?
(Mothers' Day)

P.P.S. I hope you enjoy these chocolates. We made them with the new OT.

Group Therapy Homework:

Parts of my body I am happy with: ???????

• bellybutton (I much prefer innies to outties)
• fingernails
• earlobes
• big toe on right foot (the left toe has a touch of toenail fungus)

Parts I am not happy with:
(Do you have a spare couple of hours?!)

Dear Jo,

I'm writing on behalf of Dad. He says to ask you
PLEASE, PLEASE can he come and see you.
Cause he only wants to talk.

>Love from,
>Matt

P.S. Sushi had kittens last week. She had them in
the wardrobe and they came slithering out like
rats. Yuck! And they can't see, either. Dad says
their eyes won't open for ages. There are three
tabbies and one that's black with a white nose.
The other black and white one died before it got
born. We don't know what sex they are yet. Dad's
had a look but he says they're too little.

Dear Matt,

Sorry, but I can't write to Dad. I just can't.
   You can write though. I'd love that.

Dear Issy,

I saw a doctor yesterday. He told me that if I kept
starving my body of protein it would start using muscles
for energy. (Sounds like an interesting science experiment.) He also told me that my heart wasn't functioning
properly due to all the throwing up. I think that's part of
their strategy – to frighten us into eating.

Trouble is – I think my battery's run out, Issy. Well,
that's how it feels. Like my insides have frozen and everything's ground to a halt. It all takes so much effort. Even
thinking is exhausting. It's hard to explain but it's like
part of me has shrivelled up inside.

The last few days have been crap. I'm just lying here
doing nothing, like a blob of yuck. Like a cup of cold sick.
'A cup of cold sick.' Where have I heard that line before?
Does it sound familiar to you?

Two days later:
The cleaning lady came yesterday and there was an
incident. She must have finally noticed Charlotte because
suddenly she had the vacuum cleaner pipe hurled way up
in the air and I had to act fast to stop poor Charlotte from
being sucked into oblivion. Luckily, I got there just in time.

Then two nurses came and put me back in bed and it
took me ages to explain and, well…

Please tell me I'm not losing it, Issy.

Dear Jo,

You are not losing it. You are going to be fine. A cup of cold sick! Yes! I do remember that line:

> *Mouldy, mouldy custard in a green snot pie,*
> *Mix it all together with a dead dog's eye.*
> *Mash it up with mustard and spread it on thick*
> *Then wash it all down with a cup of cold sick.*

I have this vague memory of chanting it for skipping. You are I were coring and poor Matt was trying to jump the rope. He was hopeless. Remember? Boys are such crap skippers.

Dear Issy,

I've been on special bed rest for ten days with no privileges at all, which includes washing my hair. I won't bore you with the details but if it hadn't been for Dot talking to me I'd have gone completely round the twist. The 'good' news is I've managed to put on two kilos, which has made everyone happy except me. I feel so revolting. Like a tub of lard.

Caroline reckons as long as we leave this place looking like over-inflated beach balls they'll be happy. I think she's right. But how can putting on ten kilos make anyone happy?

She gave me some Ketostix the other day. I'd never heard of them before. They come in a box and have these little coloured bits on the end like a match and you dip them in your pee to see if they change colour. If they turn purple it's good because that means your body is getting energy from its own fat. If they stay pink then your body is getting energy from food so you won't lose weight. I've been purple for two days now.

Missing you heaps, Issy.

Luv,

Jo

P.S. There's a very strange girl in room 22, along the corridor. I've seen her around but we've never spoken. She's usually in a wheelchair and she dresses like a Goth – black hair, black lips, nails, the works. And bare feet. Always bare feet. Very witchy-poo.

Anyway, this morning she's sitting in the lounge smoking a cigarette. Leon and I are playing Trivial Pursuit at the table. It is definitely against the rules to light up in the lounge. There are notices everywhere. You have to go right outside to smoke. So one of the nurses tells her to put out the cigarette. But she acts like she doesn't hear, staring ahead like she's in a trance. The nurse tells her again but she takes no notice. So then, the nurse takes the cigarette and stubs it out in a saucer. This girl doesn't bat an eye, even when the nurse wheels her out of the room. But as she's going out the door she yells something out. Something weird.

Leon says her name's Francine Colson and she's been in here for ages, only she's grown stranger and stranger. She got kicked out of group therapy a few weeks ago. I can't imagine why anyone would get kicked out of group therapy but Leon says she's got some pretty nutty ideas and she was always trying to stuff things up for the counsellor. Anyway, I was thinking 'Francine Colson' — why did that name sound familiar? And then I realised. Her initials are F.C. and she writes all this weird poetry.

One of F.C.'s poems:

> *'Let me be weightless and airy and light, and maybe I'll find peace tonight.'*

Or this one:

The Shape of Things
Whittle me down
As far as you can
Carve my angles tight
A work of art, a body part
Chiselled cheekbones,

Nice and thin
Wrists like twigs
Shape and trim.

Weird, huh?

Dear Jo,

Hmmnnn … those poems are pretty bizarre all right. They must have something to do with her illness.

I borrowed a book about anorexia from the school library because I thought it might help me understand. Only now I wished I'd got a nice cosy fantasy instead. Something with a good plot and a happy ending. (Or maybe I should have stuck with my usual – *The Guinness Book of Records*.)

Anyway, the book is called *Dying to be Thin* and it has five true-life stories of people with anorexia. One of the stories was about these twins called Penelope and Patricia. Apparently, Penelope was always the 'chubby one' until one day she decided she wasn't going to be the 'chubby one' any more. So, she decided to become the 'skinny one' and five years later she was dead. The story was told from Patricia's point of view, so it was like one twin watching her sister starve to death. It was so sad and I got all tearful and had to leave the class before anyone saw me blubbing.

So I read Theresa's tale in the loos. Far out! This Theresa gets so thin that her tailbone actually breaks through the skin and ... well, I didn't read any more after that because the book really freaked me out. There are photos of girls who look like famine victims. One is, like, twenty-three and looks about a hundred and ten. This disease is scary, Jo. Your kidneys fail and your hair falls out. Do you seriously want to go to the formal with no hair?!

Dear Jo,

Please ignore my last letter. I'm sure you don't need any more lectures or scare-mongering (is that the right word?).

What you need right now is gossip.

Okay ... here goes. So guess who Marko Deans is taking to the formal? I'll give you a clue. Her name starts with 'A' and she's been going out with his best friend for the past six months. (Yes. Amanda Curtis!)

You should have been there. Marko and Dave had this big scrap outside 'D' block near that purple rhodo bush. We were just coming out of maths and there they were. Marko had Dave's tie and was pulling it really tight and Dave was all red and sweaty. They were both yelling and swearing and some of the girls started squealing and

74

then Mr O'Malley came racing out of class to break them up. But they just carried on hitting and kicking like Mr O'Malley wasn't even there and you could tell he was too scared to get between them, like they were pitbulls or something. Tane Milton had to break them up in the end and they all got marched over to the principal's office.

Oh, and guess what else?! There's this new school rule. All Year Elevens have to do at least one culture option. It's the new DP's idea. Mr Stalker. Mum thinks the sun shines out of that guy's bum, but that's another story. Anyway … I've joined the school newspaper. Yes, me! Don't laugh. It was a choice between choir, kapa haka, debating, or newspaper, and deciding which one I'd hate least. After serious consideration I figured that 'newspaper' was the only one that didn't involve standing on a stage making a complete dork of myself. I know I'm useless at writing but I'm hoping to get a job as photographer, which might be good for a laugh and could also be a possible career option providing I steer clear of self-timing units and try not to chop everyone's heads off.

Most of the others are from Year Twelve. There are two issues per month and we meet once a week on Tuesdays in the library. Doesn't sound too daunting. I'll keep you posted.

Not much else to report on the school front. In English, we've started reading *A Slipping Down Life* by Ann Tyler. I'm up to page 88, which is pretty good for me. We were having this discussion in English the other day. One of the characters in the book – Evie – gets a guy's name tattooed on her forehead. (And his name is Drumstrings Casey!!) Well, Miss Haddock was talking about tattoos and stuff and Sarah Woodrow starts giggling down the back of the room. So Miss Haddock says what's so funny and would she like to share it with the rest of us. And guess what? Well, Sarah rolls up her sleeve and shows the whole class this tattoo, which is like a proper tattoo of a heart with someone's name in it. SAM F.! And it's real. Sarah Woodrow?!! SAM F.! Can you believe it? Absolutely the last person on earth you would ever imagine with a tattoo! And who the heck is Sam F.?

Luv,
Issy

P.S. I found this joke book at a sale at Paper Plus in the weekend and I thought it might cheer you up. Read the one on page 13!

Dear Issy,

You?! Working on the school newspaper?! I don't believe it! Next thing you'll be signing up for library duty, buying 'save the whale' badges and hugging pine trees.

Hey, thanks for the joke book.

These are my favourites so far.

A bloke loses his dog. 'Put an ad in the paper,' says a friend. So he does. A little classified reading, 'Here boy!'

How do crazy people go through the forest? They take the psycho path.

What do prisoners use to call each other? Cell phones.

What lies at the bottom of the ocean and twitches? A nervous wreck.

Leon put the one about the mental health hotline on the noticeboard:

If you are obsessive/compulsive, press 1 repeatedly.
If you have multiple personalities, press 5,6,7 and 8.
If co-dependent, please ask someone to press 2 for you.
If you are paranoid, stay on the line so we can trace your call.
If you are having a nervous breakdown, please fiddle with the # key.
If you have low self-esteem, please hang up. All of our operators are too busy to bother with you...

A couple of nurses raised their eyebrows at that. And mean old Morag took it down. Dot says not to take it personally because Morag has absolutely no sense of humour.

Dot is really cool, Issy. Some of the others don't talk to you much. One really looks down her nose at us, in fact – but Dot's great. She treats me like a proper human being and not some screwed-up teenager. And she tells me stuff about her own life as well. She's probably not supposed to do that but she does and, I know it sounds weird, but it really helps to hear about other people's problems sometimes.

You get pretty self-centred in here and you forget about normal people having issues. Like, Dot is on this anti-male rampage after discovering that her husband had been cheating for the past five years. And not only that but most of her friends knew and didn't bother telling her. Gutted! Dot thinks that even her own daughter might have known about it. She asked me the other day what I'd do if I knew my dad was cheating on my mum. Would I tell? I said I didn't know. For a start, I couldn't imagine Dad doing that in the first place but I guess you never know. I don't think Dot thought it would happen either. What would you do?

Dot's favourite joke is on page 156:

Two women are having lunch together and discussing the merits of cosmetic surgery.

The first woman says, 'I need to be honest with you, I'm getting a boob job.'

The second woman says, 'Oh, that's nothing. I'm thinking of having my arsehole bleached.'
To which the first replies, 'I just can't picture your husband blond!'

I felt bad when I read your last letter, Issy. That sounds like a very depressing book to me and it pays not to believe everything you read. My tailbone is not going to come through my skin and I am definitely not going to die. I'm sure they exaggerate these things to sell books. I bet they had something really gruesome and eye-catching on the cover too, didn't they?

As I've already mentioned – I am the fattest person in the ward by far.

Hey, guess what. There's a swimming pool in the next building across. I only just found that out. It's a lap pool. The doctor says when I put on another 3 kilos I might be allowed to use it. I haven't swum for months. Not since you and I went to the salt-water pool on the bus that day and your wallet got stolen. Remember?! And it had all our money in it, plus all those Glasson's birthday vouchers from your sisters. We had to walk home that day. And it was nearly eight o'clock by the time we got back and Dad went crook because it was Tuesday and he'd missed his rugby game. He reckoned he was angry because he was concerned about me but I'm sure it was because of missing the rugby…

Anyway, you're not to worry because I've made some

resolutions. I've decided I'm going to try really hard from now on. And I'm going to eat everything they give me because when I get to 50 kilos they're going to let me out.

Oh well, I better go. There's a group therapy session this afternoon.

Keep writing,

Jo

Dear Jo,

Good for you. You go, girl!

Hmmmnnnnn ... Poor Dot. I don't know what I'd do in that situation. I don't think my parents have time for extra-marital activities!!! Mum has far too many meetings as it is! Don't think there'd be room in her hectic schedule for any sneaky rendezvous. I guess you never know though.

Yeah, I remember when my wallet got stolen. The ugly sisters never forgave me for losing those vouchers!

Group Therapy Homework:

Things I'm proud of doing:
- Pitching a tent in the backyard, blindfolded. (I was seven at the time and it was for a Brownie badge and I was the only one who got it right first time.)
- Swimming the whole length of the school pool underwater.
- Completing 40 hr famine and raising $48.60 for Ethiopia.

Good things about my personality:
- I am honest (usually).
- I say what I think (mostly).
- I have good will power.

Not so good things about my personality:
- I hold a grudge.
- I have a bad temper (sometimes).
- I say what I think (aka having a big gob).

Dear Jo,

Meredith hates my formal dress. She thinks it's the wrong colour and makes my bum look fat. She hates the bells, too, I can tell. Not that she comes out and says so. Oh no, she'd rather keep dropping these subtle hints. Like,

'Are redheads supposed to wear purple?' And 'Have you thought about joining the gym, Issy?' And, 'Would you like a go on my new rebounder?'

No thanks, Meredith, I'll just stay the way Mother Nature intended. She hates me saying that cause as you know she's exactly the same build as me and would rather waste her life fighting against Mother Nature's intentions. The fact is – big hips and thighs are part of the Muirhead gene pool. You've only got to look at Mum and Dad to see where I come from. And Meredith!

Make the most of what you've got and cover the rest with a baggy top, that's my theory.

Dear Issy,

You are definitely the wisest person I know and I think you should hire yourself out as a professional cheerer-upper.

    Luv,

    Jo

P.S. 'Make the most of what you've got and cover the rest with a baggy top.' I like that. Might put it on our notice-board. Does that go for baggy bottoms as well?

Dear Diary,

First I'd like to make it absolutely clear that this is absolutely not my idea. Blame the new OT. As well as making homemade chocolates, she thinks keeping a journal will be 'beneficial for my recovery'. I told her I am not the journal keeping type but sometimes it's easier to go with the flow and I don't have the energy for aggro these days.

So I agreed, but only if she promised that no one can read it without my permission. You have to be careful about stuff like that. Issy's cousin, Laura, kept a journal once. She had a crush on this boy from St Paul's called Russell Richmond and she wrote all this stuff in her diary about him. But then her mother read it and freaked out. She acted like Laura was a raving nymphomaniac and wouldn't let her out of the house for months.

I thought that was so unfair. It should have been the mother who was grounded for being such a nosey old cow.

Jo

Hi Sis,

It's me, Matt!

Dad thought it would be a good idea for me to write you a letter. He says I have to write at least one page, which is why the letters are so big. As you know I'm not that great at writing but I'll give it a go. Please excuse any spelling mistakes. Today is sunny. I hope it is sunny at your hospital. This term at school we are doing food technology, which is the same as cooking but they think boys will like it more if it's called technology. Dumb, eh. Cooking is cooking and it's much better than maths, whatever they want to call it – because at least you get to eat.

Anyway, on Monday we made Weetbix Delight, which is yummy and doesn't take much technology to make. I put a sample in this letter for you to eat. Hope it's not too squashed.

Recipe for Weetbix Delight
3 crushed Weetbix
1 cup coconut
4 oz butter, melted
1 cup flour
1 cup sugar
1 tsp baking powder
Add melted butter to dry ingredients. Press

into sponge roll tin. Bake 15 mins in moderate oven.

Get well soon,
Luv Matt

Dear Diary,

Okay, where to start? This is so embarrassing, like going on a date or something. Not that I've been on an actual date. Well, not a proper one. Last year I went to the movies with a guy called Todd Pritchard. It was some James Bond thing. Anyway, things were going okay until half time when he asked if I wanted an ice cream. I said 'no thanks' but he bought me one anyway. Probably thought I was just being polite, except that polite is not really my style. I'm more of a straight talker. If you don't want something, say so – that's my theory. So I did. And when he came back with two ice creams I said it again. 'No thanks.' (Well, I hadn't eaten anything for two days and I wasn't about to ruin it for his benefit!) So then he had to sit there eating both ice creams, which served him right really but was kind of embarrassing for both of us. We didn't talk much after that and he never asked me to the movies again. Or anywhere else, actually. Wonder why?!

So …

My name is Johanna Margaret Morrison.
Margaret was my grandmother's name but she's
dead just now. She was eighty when she died
(which everyone said was a good innings) and had
no distinguishing features apart from a fetish for
crocheted doilies. (When she died they found 164
stacked in her hall cupboard. So Mum and Aunty
Kay got half each.)

Anyway, I'm fifteen years old. They tell me I've
got anorexia but they tell everyone in here the
same thing. They're into labels. And they want us
all to get fat and roly poly out of here. Ye hah! But
fat doesn't mean happy, does it? Take poor Dot for
example. She's put on eight kilos because of what
her slimey husband did behind her back.

Anyway, most of the patients in here are piles
skinnier than I am.

I used to eat loads but now food makes me ill so
I have to vomit, which is pretty disgusting, I know.
But I can't help it, which is why it's better not eating in the first place. It's easy once you get used to
it. I can go without food for days. Eating makes me
feel, like, so out of control. My favourite food used
to be KFC. I could eat a whole five piece pack all
by myself, plus potato and gravy, chips and a large
Coke. I'd die if I had to eat one now. I feel sick just
writing about it. Have you seen how much fat
drips out of that stuff??!! Did you know that one

steak and cheese pie has a golf ball of fat in it?

Sometimes I think that if I started eating again I might never stop. And I might end up like Dot (who is a really nice person but a bit on the plump side).

Well, that's all you're getting for today.

Bye,

Jo

Dear Issy,

Why do bagpipers walk when they play? They're trying to get away from the noise. Ha. Ha.

I think that's what I'm doing in here, trying to get away from the noise. Except that it's not working. But maybe I brought my own noise with me because usually the noise in my head is rowdier than anything outside. Sometimes it feels like pot lids crashing together with me stuck in the middle. Matt used to drive Mum mental when he got into the pot cupboard and started crashing about. She didn't do anything to stop him though, just lay on the couch with her hands covering her ears. Either that or she'd take herself off to bed and leave me to deal with it.

All this writing I'm doing, yet I still feel like I'm going round and round in circles. I may as well tell you now, Issy. I'm not going to make it to the formal. It's not going to happen. Please don't be too mad.

Tell Mrs Hopkins the virus has mutated (is that the right word?). I know I've let you down, Issy, and I'm really sorry. But I figured if I let you know in plenty of time you could get someone else to double date with and to be honest I'm pretty crap company at the moment so I'd probably ruin it for you, anyway.

Hey ... fancy Marko Deans asking Amanda. No wonder Dave S. had him swinging by the necktie. Some guys have the morals of a spider (especially the ones at Cameron College) and I think you did right getting a blind date. I know I was against the idea in the beginning but surely he can't be any worse than a dickhead from our school.

So ... how is the posh frock coming along? Lucky your mum is such a great seamstress. I think purple will be stunning with your red hair and don't let that Meredith put you off. She's always had a bit of a jealous streak.

Not much has been happening here lately. A new girl called Pip arrived last week. Poor thing. She looks totally petrified – like a mouse with a twitchy nose and little pink eyes. She has this posh accent and wears expensive pink clothes. Even the braces on her teeth are pink! She and Ingrid seem to get on okay though, which is good.

Yesterday Leon asked if she'd like to play Trivial Pursuit and she looked like he'd just asked her to get naked or something. I thought she was going to scamper up the bookcase in fright. Pity! It'd be good to have an extra player. I get sick of always coming last.

Still, at least it gives us an excuse to chat. Leon isn't

exactly what you'd call a 'chatterbox' but sometimes when we're playing Trivial Pursuit he really opens up. Like the other day he told me some stuff about his family. He has an older sister who's studying to be a doctor and his mum is a high-powered executive type who trains staff for (wait for it ...) Jenny Craig! Somehow I don't think having an anorexic son would be great for business. (Or maybe it would.) Anyway, his dad left them a few months ago and he and Leon don't get on. I get the feeling his dad isn't too keen on Leon being gay. Not that he said so. Well, actually Leon hasn't said anything about being gay, either. But I think it's highly possible and, like I said, he's certainly got the voice for it.

Mind you, one thing I've learned from being in here is that appearances can be deceptive. Also, you never know what goes on inside other people's heads.

For example – Kara came by my room the other day. She's the Asian girl – very shy and nervous. Her nails are bitten right down so raw that sometimes they bleed. Anyway, she's sitting on my bed looking like she has something really important to say.

'There's something I need to tell you, Jo,' she says.

'Okay. Fire away, Kara.'

Then she takes a deep breath and my heart is like pounding in anticipation for what's coming next.

'That painting's crooked,' she says.

'Sorry?'

'That painting's crooked.' Then she walks over to

my lighthouse, straightens the painting (which wasn't crooked in the first place) and wanders off.

Like I said, you never know what's going on inside people's heads and usually it's not nearly as interesting as you think.

Keep writing.

Luv,

Jo

Dear Diary,

I've just come back from a group session. Veronica
wanted us to talk about the progress we're making.
No one said much. Kara picked at her jumper and
kept her feet in perfectly correct alignment; Ingrid
was a hundred miles away (probably on some
imaginary training run or other) and Pip just
stared out the window. Leon jiggled his right leg,
chewed his lip and looked totally pissed off.

'Is there something you'd like to share with us,
Leon?' says Veronica.

Leon chewed his lip some more and jiggled a
bit harder.

'We're waiting, Leon.'

And then the sparks started to fly. 'What is it
with you guys?' he snapped and Veronica looked
gobsmacked.

'Pardon?'

'You never know when to let up, do you? You're
always harping on at us about making progress.
Getting better. Nag. Nag. Nag.'

'Well, er ...'

'Has it ever crossed your mind that some of us
might be happy as we are? That, well, maybe we
don't want to make progress.' (He said the word
'progress' with a real sarcastic whine in his voice.)

'Are you happy as you are, Leon?'

'Maybe.'

'Really?'

He thought about it, then said 'Yeah, well … who says I'd be any happier if I was fat?'

'But the goal isn't to get fat, Leon.' Veronica was back in full therapist mode now. 'The goal is to get healthy – functioning at a healthy weight. It's not normal to –'

'And who gets to define this healthy weight exactly?' – Leon.

'A healthy weight is when your kidneys aren't collapsing.' – Veronica. 'A healthy weight is when your potassium levels are normal and your bowels are functioning.'

'You just want to take control,' – Leon. 'This is the only thing we have left and you want to take it away…'

'Have you seen Francine lately?' – Veronica. 'Have you seen what being in control has done for her?'

'She's doing what she wants to do, isn't she?' – Leon. 'It's a free world, isn't it?'

'Do you really believe that, Leon?'

I tried talking to Leon later because I wanted to make sure he was okay. And also because I was interested in what he said about having control. Because that's how I feel sometimes. I guess I wondered if he felt the same as me. What he said was interesting: 'When I first stopped eating it was like I was taking a stand. Taking control of something. It annoyed the hell out of Mum but she couldn't do anything about it. I guess I quite liked that. It was me in charge for once.'

'Are you still in charge now, then?' I asked him.

He couldn't answer that. He just shrugged like he wasn't sure of anything any more.

We played Trivial Pursuit after tea. TP questions are totally random and utterly impossible.

P.S. Example! *What did Joe Cocker buy for $60 in Sydney in October, 1972?*

Marijuana.

Friggin' idiot!!!

Dear Diary,

'Dear Diary' – How corny is that. Sounds like a little kid about to spill her secrets, which is strange because when I woke up this morning I was a little kid again – back home in Cutler Street. It was weird. Surreal. Like Mum and Dad were in the kitchen making breakfast and I was sitting at the table dribbling golden syrup onto my porridge and licking the spoon. Mum looked amazing. Like she was Mum, but she wasn't – if you know what I mean. Then she picked out the shiniest apple from the bowl to put in my lunchbox and she was smiling. (Kind of oddly.) Then Dad pecked her cheek and said 'Bye, Honey' (just like on the tele). And the sky was blue and the sun was shining and all was well with the world.

But when I woke up I was in a hospital bed and

the sky was grey and it was pissing down with rain. And there was a sick feeling in my tummy, knowing that breakfast was in the common room in half an hour. I so dread meal times. Skiddling scrambled egg around my plate for hours. Being under constant surveillance … Honestly, this place can be so suffocating.

Leon and Caroline had a ripper argument this afternoon.

Caroline was watching Oprah on TV3 and Leon kept changing channels. We all have him on about liking the 'Bob' cartoons. His favourite is *Bob the Builder* but he's quite fond of *Sponge Bob* too. Anyway, Caroline got up and changed it back, which was when the argument started.

Leon – 'I don't know how you can watch that rubbish. It's pathetic navel-gazing crap.'

Caroline – 'You can talk – cartoon man…'

Oprah – 'We're having a "girls' party" today.' Big toothy grin.

Then Leon rolls his eyes and says 'A girls' party, huh!' and changes back to *Sponge Bob Square Pants*. On the tele, a girl called Melissa is telling Oprah all about how she lost her virginity at sixteen. 'I slept with everyone in sight and had to change schools,' she says, which for some reason gets right up Leon's nose.

'Don't tell us your problems lady,' he says.

'Melissa is obviously hungry for something,' says Oprah, oblivious to the trouble brewing in a psych ward on the other side of the world. 'And, as women, we have to start filling ourselves up with things that make us feel whole and valuable, not worthless and cheap.' (Or something to that effect.)

'Give us a break!' says Leon, which prompts Caroline to hurl a coffee cup at him. (Polystyrene, luckily.)

'Have a heart, arsehole,' she says.

'A lot of young girls treat their bodies like trash cans...' Oprah continues.

'Well, that's their bloody lookout,' says Leon.

'And men will drop their trash in our bodies if we let them –' says Oprah.

That's when Leon stomps out.

And Caroline, looking all surprised, says, in this really childish voice: 'What's burning his biscuits today, Jo?'

How the heck should I know? But I guess it doesn't take a rocket scientist to figure out that Leon must feel pretty outnumbered by females in here.

Two days later:
I think Veronica must watch Oprah as well – to get ideas, I mean.

Today she asked us what we would wish for if our fairy godmother appeared. But don't hold your breath for anything earth-shattering. Kara just shrugged her shoulders and didn't wish for anything. Pip wished she could make her mum and dad happy, which was just about the saddest and most pathetic thing I'd ever heard. (Even sadder knowing that she meant it.)

Ingrid bit her lip and looked like she was going to burst into tears, as usual.

Leon said he'd like to write a song for Bob Dylan to sing, which I thought was pretty awesome. And at least he'd thought about it. As for me, my mind went completely blank. Well, there was one thing.

Veronica perked up. 'And what's that, Jo?'

I looked down at the floor because I was too scared to say it out loud. Too scared to hear my own voice crack. 'To have Mum back,' I said.

Must go,

Jo

Dear Issy,

Did you know that a spider has an exoskeleton that she has to shed in order to grow? Creepy, huh? Which explains why you see those headless spider bodies lying about on windowsills. Although, when you think about it shedding your own body is actually quite a cool concept. A good chance to start again.

Speaking of which ... I had an interesting conversation with Dot last night. We were talking about people reinventing themselves and how amazing it would be to start your life over – like slipping into a new skin. Dot said the first thing she'd change would be her name. She reckons 'Dot' is kind of inappropriate for someone who weighs 98 kilos. I guess she has a point. 'They would've been better off calling me "Blob",' she says. Poor Dot.

Dear Mum,

Two fat blokes are in a pub. One says to the other, 'Your round.'
The other says: 'So are you, you fat git.'

My best friend, Issy, sent me a joke book. She knows it's hard work being gifted and talented and ~~hospital~~ camp can be hard going especially when everyone at school is gearing up for the major event of the year, which is the senior formal dance. Gifted and talented people take themselves very seriously. Well, I guess they have to, because no one else does.

Luv,
Jo

Group Therapy Homework:

Things I can do without:
- Fat thighs
- Group therapy
- KFC

Things I can't do without:
- Throwing up
- Anorexia
- Issy's letters

Things I fear:
- Death by starvation
- Bird flu
- Going back to school
- Car crashes
- Opening my big gob

Dear Sis,

This week we made pizza. I had to wrap mine in
loo paper (unused!) because Martin Wainwright
used the last paper napkin. I hope you like it. It
will taste better if you heat it in the microwave
first. (Twenty seconds on high should do it. Dad
and I are getting good at the microwave now.)
Do they have microwaves there?

Sorry there's no cheese but Martin Wainwright used the last of that as well. So I put on
more chilli sauce instead.

Luv,
Matt

Recipe for Pizza

Make scone dough. Roll into a ball. Then roll
out flat. Spread on chilli sauce. Add other stuff,
like pineapple, bacon and cheese. Bake in hot
oven until cooked.

Yum!

P.S. Thanks for that spider stuff. Cool.
P.P.S. Poor Mrs Ramsay got done for shoplifting
again. It said in the paper that she pinched a
garden fork from K-Mart, which Dad says is
really silly cause she could buy herself a million
garden forks if she wanted to.

Dear Matt,

Thanks for the pizza. It was perfect, especially the crust, which was nice and crunchy.

How is Sushi? How is Mrs Jordan?

I hope you are working hard at school.

Luv,

Jo

P.S. I think you need to do something about that Martin Wainwright.

P.P.S. Give Sushi a pat for me and tell her congratulations about the kittens.

P.P.P.S. Re: Mrs Ramsay — sometimes people do the strangest things, don't they? And for no apparent reason.

Dear Jo,

What say I just come visit for half an hour? We need to talk. I've spoken with the doctor and he thinks so too.

Please, Jo. Please let me visit.

Missing you heaps,

Love always,

Dad

Toilet Graffiti:

All we have left is the power to refuse.

D,

(Sounds slightly better than 'dear diary' – more direct and less flowery.) To the point. That's me.

Today I feel sick.

Sick of being inside my own head. It's such a mess in here. A stuffed up mess. They nag at me to eat but I'm scared because I know that once I start I won't be able to stop. I'll just eat and eat and eat until I burst like a big fat bubble.

Like the first time I binged.

It was because of Aunty Kay. Well, it wasn't actually her fault or anything. But she was staying with us. Aunty Kay is Mum's sister. I mean WAS Mum's sister. (No, that's not right either. Are you still someone's sister if they die?)

Anyway, she had this new baby called Zak and they came to stay with us for the weekend, which I really hated. I'm not even sure why. I just felt crap with everyone playing happy families. Like I was in the way. Aunty Kay is so different since she's had the baby. It's weird. Everyone wanted to hold it except for me. That's all they wanted to do. Even Matt. What a fuss. Like, he had to sit on the couch with cushions propped up everywhere and the baby's head had to be exactly right and it was all a big drama with Uncle Brian taking photos every time the baby even opened its mouth. Then, when it pooed, it was some, like, major medical emergency.

Fuss. Fuss. Fuss. Dad said Zak looked just like Matt did when he was a baby, which isn't surprising considering everyone says how much Aunty Kay looks like Mum. Dad said a lot of stuff that weekend. He was getting all nostalgic and I guess it made me feel guilty.

It felt weird watching Aunty Kay with the baby too. Hard to explain. I guess I felt confused and … jealous, maybe. And when they left I felt sad. And then I felt guilty again.

And that's when I started pigging out. I was cleaning up after dinner and instead of putting the leftovers in the fridge I put them straight in my mouth. We'd had spaghetti bolognaise and garlic bread and I just stuffed everything in. Packed it all down my neck. And once I started I couldn't stop. It was like I'd found this hole and I was plugging it up with food.

When I finished I felt sick and full and disgusting – like a big fat pig. And I had to go lie down on the bed because I felt so revolting and then I thought 'if only I could get rid of it'. And that's when I made myself sick. That's the first

time I ever put my fingers down my throat… The first
time ever…

Must write to Issy again soon.

D,
God, I hate hospitals!

The smell of disinfectant – everything all stiff and
starchy. It's like being cut off from the world, because
when you look out the window people are just going
about their business without you. And you think, how
dare they? How dare they carry on like that without you?
It's like no one even knows you're up there – all flattened
into nothing, with starched sheets and nurses and doctors
telling you what to do all day. I feel like taking one of
those stupid sheets and writing 'Help!' in big fat letters
with orange lipstick or tomato sauce or something and
dangling it out the window. Except that there are all these
humungously high hedges everywhere so probably no
one would even notice. Maybe that's why they grew the
hedges in the first place. Maybe there have been escape
missions in the past with patients abseiling to freedom on
knotted hospital sheets…

Nah!

It was scary when Mum went into hospital. At first
Dad said it was going to be for just the one night. Only
it wasn't because she stayed for weeks. Aunty Kay wasn't
married then so she came to help look after us.

I remember going to visit Mum with Dad and Aunty Kay. She was propped up in bed with pillows – a red cardy draped around her shoulders, her hair sticking out funny and no lipstick on. Slow motion Mum with this weird slurry voice and dead-bird eyes.

Two days later:
Francine has got worse. I don't know the details but apparently her family are at her bedside, so it must be serious.

Poor things. It must be hard when there's nothing you can do to help. When all you can do is stand and watch.

Like with Mum. God, I hated it. All those creepy corridors and the nurses making silly jokes and talking to her like she was some little kid. 'How are we today, Mrs Morrison? We won't get big and strong if we don't eat our breakfast, will we now?'

The meals came on a trolley. Dry knobs of food plonked on thick white plates. How could she eat that muck? We're not allowed meals on trolleys in this hospital because we have to eat in the dining room with knives and forks and nurses watching on like hawks. Not much fun for them either, I don't suppose. (Watching Kara eat is excruciating. She cuts every piece of food into a zillion tiny mouthfuls, stacking it all into little piles.) The rest of us aren't much better, chewing the meat until it turns to dust in our mouths. In this place you can't leave the table until thirty minutes after you eat. That's the rule.

At Mum's hospital I pressed the wrong button in the lift once and we ended up on this floor that was like a museum with glass cases full of old surgical instruments and stuff. They looked more like tools for fixing cars to me. I used to have nightmares about those instruments.

Mum had electric shock treatment. Bzzzzz … Bzzzz …

I wasn't supposed to know that but Aunty Kay let it slip one day when we were having a milkshake at the hospital café. Electric shocks were going to make her better, she said. Electric shocks? How bizarre. I used to imagine the doctors forcing her fingers into the electric plug and her hair standing on end like in the cartoons.

When Mum came home from hospital she was a different person. She didn't lie about in bed all day any more but she was like a robot. Dad said it was the drugs and just 'give it a couple of months and she'll be right as rain'. But she looked so vacant, like no one was home. Even her hair looked weird and when she smiled it was only her mouth because her eyes were blank holes. Blankety blank. Everything in slow motion. Hey, Mum. Knock, knock. Who's there?

'Go away and leave me alone.'

She didn't get mad like she used to. She didn't cover her ears or lose her temper or slouch off to the bedroom when Matt played with the pots any more. Nothing like that. The trouble was, she didn't get anything. She just smiled this fake robot smile and cleaned the house. One day I watched her cleaning the bench. Wipe, wipe, wipe with the dishcloth on the same spot, over and over, gazing into nothingland. *Where are you, Mum?* I wanted to scream. *Where the heck are you?*!!!

Her pills were in a line on the windowsill above the sink. Dad used to say if they tipped her up she'd rattle. He tried to make a joke of it but it was hard to laugh.

The pills made her fat and her face went into a different shape – like a potato. They made her forget things, too. Important things. Like, one day she forgot to pick me up from school. In the junior school you're not allowed to leave until someone collects you. And because Mum didn't arrive I had to stay on the mat until the last kid left and then Mrs Clayton took me to the office and phoned home. She waited for ages, tapping her long nails on the desk and pursing her lips to let me know she had more important things to do – looking at her watch every two seconds. But there was no answer. So then she phoned Dad's work and he came racing over – grumpy, but pretending not to be.

At home Mum was fast asleep on the couch with Matt crying his head off in his bedroom. Matt's face was blotchy red like he'd been bawling for hours but Mum hadn't heard a thing.

Dad was really mad at first but he soon calmed down. When Mum woke up she burst into tears. I had a sore tummy after that – every day my tummy felt like something bad was about to happen.

106

Dad tried to explain. He said that Mum still wasn't well and that she felt sad most of the time, which I didn't understand. Why was she sad? I had so many questions. Like why and how come and when was she going to get better?

Dad couldn't answer most of them. He said it had something to do with having the baby, so I asked if she was sad after having me as well and Dad said yes, a little bit, and I said well, what did she go and have another baby for then?

And Dad just shrugged.

Some days were better than others. Some days Mum seemed fine and others were write-offs. She couldn't cope with anything going wrong.

Like, for example, not long after Mum came home from hospital our fridge broke down. We got home from school and the ice cream was all melted and the frozen veg were soggy and there was blood dripping from the mince. So we took everything out, put it on the bench and waited for Dad to come home. Dad said there was no point mucking around because once a fridge broke down it was just as cheap to get a new one. So we all traipsed into town to choose a new fridge. The man said the new fridge would be delivered the next day and they'd take the old one away for nothing.

When I got home from school the next day I couldn't wait to see our new fridge. I'd been thinking about it all day. But Mum was sitting at the table with her head in her hands like something bad had happened. And there were two fridges in the kitchen – the new one and the old one. Side by side. I asked her why they hadn't taken the broken fridge away and she said they didn't take it away because there turned out to be nothing wrong with it. A fuse had blown, that was all, which meant there was nothing wrong with the original fridge.

I still couldn't work out why we now had two fridges. And I don't think Mum could either. She just sat there with her head in her hands like the whole world was coming to an end.

When Dad got home he just laughed. I should have checked all that out, he said. Oh well, not to worry.

Dear Jo,

Breaking news – Ashley King has broken up with Ben
Spooner. What a drama. Only two weeks to go and now
she has no partner. I'm beginning to think a blind date is
not such a bad idea after all. At least you can't have an
argument and stuff everything up. Well, not before the big
night anyway.

Hey, and guess what my first assignment for the newspaper is? A full report on the formal. I'm allowed to take
the school's digital camera along to get some candid shots,
which might be fun. And at least I'll have something to do
if it gets boring. My job is to take the pictures and there's
a Year Twelve guy called Tim who's going to do the text.
He's quite cute really, in a slightly nerdy kind of way.

Oh, and my mystery man has finally been revealed.
He's called Mike Maxwell. I feel more nervous than ever
knowing his name. Mike Maxwell? What do you think?!

We are going as a foursome with Kathy Symons and a
guy called Rodney who is Mike Maxwell's friend and Mum
says I have to start looking forward to it and stop fretting
about you not being there. (Which is all very well for her
to say!)

I don't know what Kathy Symons is like. All I know is
that she's number two on the tennis ladder and she's got
an older brother called Malcolm in Year Thirteen who
plays in the school orchestra.

Oh, one good thing: she's offered her place for

pre-formal cocktails, which gives me an excuse to get Mum off my back. I know she's been champing at the bit to do it but I'd rather keep my family on the sidelines, at arms length, and as far away from the action as possible.

Meredith is getting on my nerves and if I hear one more word about the great formal of 2000 I will run away and join a travelling science fair. You are so lucky to have a brother, Jo. Sisters are the pits, especially older ones who've done everything before you have and of course it was so much better when they did it. They both had proper dates to start with! (Not blind ones, like me.) Or, so they keep saying.

Anyway, they forget that I've actually seen their formal photos and the guys don't look that shit hot to me. Kate's wasn't too bad but the guy Meredith went with looks like something out of the new *King Kong* movie.

Must go.

Take care, Jo.

Luv, Issy

P.S. Special treat! Mum bought me make-up the other day. It was kind of like shopping for my first bra! A mother/daughter bonding session – well, so Mum kept saying, and I suppose it was quite sweet. I have to say the cosmetics department was an eye-opening experience. Far out! Do you have any idea how complicated choosing make-up is? Mascara technology would blow you away for starters. I had to choose between – volume building, double extension, lash expansion, extreme curl and wide eye. And here's me thinking it was all just black gook to make your lashes look longer. (Not that you'll get to see much from behind the glasses anyway. Kate reckons I should get contact lenses but I think I'd be too squeamish to put them in.)

P.P.S. I can absolutely identify with Dot not liking her name. I feel the same about Isabelle. Like, if I hear one more joke about 'is a bell necessary on your bike?' I'll scream. Isabelle sounds so old-fashioned and Isabella would have been much nicer. Then I could have been called Bella.

Dear Mr Morrison,

I am sorry to report that your daughter isn't making the progress we'd hoped. Unfortunately, there has been no significant weight gain and we feel there is more to Johanna's problems than we are currently aware. We understand that you are keen to visit but she refuses to see you. This must be difficult.

To make an appointment to discuss your daughter, please contact me at the phone number below.

Yours sincerely,
Neville Fraser (Dr)

Dear Jo,

This is new. It's called chocolate filled red liquo-rice. It's really yummy and cost a whole week's pocket money so please don't be sick after you eat it.

Love from,
Matt

P.S. I am doing a project on your thing at school and I got some stuff off the Internet about it. Did you know that some famous people like Mary-Kate Olsen have had anorexia nervosa? And there are loads of other movie stars and models and singers too.

The things you get are – losing weight quickly, knowing how many calories are in everything, exercising all the time and always talking about how fat you are. (I hope Mrs Jordan hasn't got it because she's always talking about how fat she is!!)

The things to help are – throwing out the scales, writing down ten things you like about yourself, going for a walk, seeing a movie, wear-ing clothes that are comfortable and accepting compliments.

Well, that's what the magazine said.
P.P.S. You are looking really nice today, Jo.

Mary-Kate and Anorexia

While we, like many of you, are upset that we didn't get the chance to see Mary-Kate and Ashley here in New Zealand this July, we're very happy that Mary-Kate is now getting help and is on the road to recovery…

Ashley says, 'I am very proud of my sister Mary-Kate for dealing with her problem. She is in a safe and nurturing environment and getting well. We have been incredibly touched by the tremendous outpouring of support and understanding from our friends, colleagues and fans around the world…

'Mary-Kate did a very brave thing by admitting there was something wrong with her and she needed help. It can be very difficult to admit you need help, so we admire her for that. We hope other girls who might also be suffering from this illness will be inspired to take Mary-Kate's lead and reach out for help.'

Dear Matt,

Thanks for all the information and also for the chocolate, which was totally delicious and I promise I wasn't sick after it because you're right, that would be a waste. Did you get that Martin Wainwright guy sorted out yet? I don't think it's fair that someone should have first dibs on the cheese and paper towels in your cooking (whoops, I mean food technology!) class. Does he have some secret deal going with the teacher?

How are the kittens doing? Do they have names yet and do they still look like rats? I miss Sushi a lot but I do have a spider in my room, which is nice. Her name is Charlotte. Not quite as much fun as Sushi but she's interesting to watch.

Hope you are well.

Luv,

Jo

P.S. Why don't you do a project on spiders? That'd be far more interesting. For example, did you know that spiders have lived on this earth for more than three hundred million years?

Dear Issy,

I feel like I'm stuck in some weird movie. Some days don't
feel real. Like, I'm trapped and I don't know how to get
out of my own way. When I feel like this it's comforting
to know that you are out there carrying on with your
normal life – going to Science, getting fed up with
Meredith, doing Pilates, eating sausage rolls and stuff.
I know it sounds barmy but I would give anything to be
normal again. I just don't know where to start.

Untitled
Drunk on water,
high on air
reduce
refine
dissolve
maybe even disappear
like shadows
or whispers
or echoes in the night.

F.C.

D,

Post-natal depression. That's what Mum had. That was her label. Post-natal depression? It sounded like something off the weather forecast to me.

It's funny how your memory works. I mean, there must be a hundred million moments stored inside your head but you remember only a few. That's the weird part – like, which bits do you remember and why? And how can two people from the same family have completely different memories of the same event? Like, Matt doesn't remember any of the yucky things about Mum at all. Why is that? Maybe he's just a nicer person than I am.

The question is: is it because you're a happy person to start with that you only remember the happy things or is it because you focus on the happy things that you become happy? Huh??!!

I was five when Matt was born and nine when Mum left home, which means she must have been sick for about four years. But there were good times as well.

Like when we borrowed Mrs Jordan's caravan and went camping, for example. It was during the Christmas holidays and Dad had time off work and the weather was brilliant – hot and sunny every day. We parked the caravan near a river and set up camp by these willow trees. Dad strung some rope between the trees to dry the clothes and we had this real dinky bath that he made using the chilly bin and a plastic bag. And it didn't rain once during the whole week except for a tiny little bit at night. I only remember that because Dad kept skiting about it afterwards. There was no one else around, except for us and a couple of fishermen on the other side of the river, and I wanted that holiday to go on forever and ever.

Mum read magazines in her deckchair with sun cream on her nose while Matt slept in his cot in the awning. And Dad took me fishing with the rod I got for Christmas. He caught a rainbow trout one day, but it didn't look that colourful to me. (There I go again – expecting too much as usual.) One day he took me down the river on our Lilo. We went for miles and miles just drifting along until we got to the bridge and then the current got too strong so we had to walk back. But it took ages walking and I lost my jandal and …

Anyway, when we got back Mum had all the washing done. She was proud of that – having all the washing done and the potatoes peeled.

We cooked all our food on the barbeque and Dad made these cute ring things to cook the eggs in by cutting the ends off a fish tin. I remember Mum saying she could live there full-time if she had to and Dad laughing and kissing the top of her head.

One night, after tea, Dad took me eeling. We waded through the long grass, over to the bridge. Then we found a good spot, dropped the bait in and watched. But the water was so dark and deep that I couldn't wait to get back to the caravan. I held Dad's hand tight and was glad we didn't catch any eels. I really don't think I could've swum there again if we had. In fact, I still shiver when I think about that water.

Dear Jo,

The senior formal is tomorrow night. Mum has just taken up the hem on my dress. This is what the finished product looks like. Wish me luck,
     Issy

Dear Issy,

Your posh frock looks stunning. You will look gorgeous
and the formal will be utterly fabulously fantastic. Don't
forget I want ALL the gory details!!! Every single one.
    Good luck.
    Luv,
    Jo

Dear Mum,

Do you remember that holiday we had in Mrs Jordan's
caravan?

D,
Do you know what it's like to be nine years old? All you
want is to be the same as everyone else. So, when you
bring your friends home you don't want your mum carked
out, red-eyed, on the couch, do you? And you don't want
her arriving at the school cake stall with burnt muffins,
either. Well, I didn't.
    Yesterday Leon and I were talking about mothers. He
reckons I should be grateful that Mum even bothered to
try because his Mum was always at work – too busy for

anything. I felt bad after that. He's right, you know. I really am an ungrateful cow.

D,

One day last year Aunty Kay came down again from Timaru with Uncle Brian and baby Zak. This time we all went to McDonald's for lunch. Zak sat in his high chair chucking chips everywhere, which, for some reason, everyone thought was hilarious. I tried to ignore how happy they all were. I tried to ignore the way Dad looked at Aunty Kay too, like he was thinking about someone else. I tried to ignore everything and concentrate on food.

That day I ate two double cheeseburgers and then asked Dad for a giant ice cream sundae with double chocolate sauce. That day Aunty Kay said, 'You've got a real sweet tooth, Jo, just like your mum.' I remember her saying it 'just like your mum'. She probably meant it as a compliment.

But that night, after everyone went to bed, I nicked a packet of TimTams from the cupboard and a family-sized block of Caramellow chocolate that Dad got for his birthday and half a packet of corn chips we were saving for nachos. Then I shut myself in my bedroom and ate the lot.

Then I spewed it all up again.

Group Therapy Homework:

Throwing up – Why do I do it?
   Because I can't stop.

Why shouldn't I do it?
   Because I can't stop.

Dear Jo,

You asked for all the gory details so here they are.

I am lying in bed and the Cameron College Formal is now officially over. The digital clock says 4:37 but I haven't been to sleep yet because I keep going over the night in my mind, trying to figure out what happened. You were right about the blind date thing, Jo, and I should have listened. I mean, what was I thinking? Going to a dance with some complete stranger. What kind of a nutso idea was that?

This is what happened: Mike Maxwell arrived to pick me up at 6:30, and guess what – he was totally drop dead gorgeous. I'm not kidding, Jo – when he walked in I nearly died. Olive skin, jet-black hair – the works! Meredith's eyes were on stalks, Kate was grinning like a moron and even Mum was tipped off balance a little.

Of course Dad had to go and make some embarrassing comment about me being the Belle of the Ball. 'Is-a-belle of the ball – ha, ha, ha.'

I almost chickened out there and then, Jo. Because suddenly I realised what a bad idea this blind date thing was and what the heck was I going to say to him and well, you know. Major nerve attack in progress.

Anyway, he had a flower to pin on my dress and when he leaned forward my heart was going bang-bang-bang and if he couldn't hear it then he must be deaf. But I knew exactly what he was thinking. Like, 'Hmmnnn ... this is different from what I expected ... fat, with freckles and glasses, eh. Wonder if it's too late to swap?' He didn't say that of course. Oh no, he was the model of cool, charming the pants off everyone in sight.

His friend Rodney was waiting outside, with the car engine running, so there was no time for idle chitchat. Unfortunately, this didn't stop Mum delivering her usual lecture on the evils of drink-driving and the reasons why I was the only chick in school who had to be home by twelve-thirty. (I've told her a thousand times that no one else gets home before daylight but she can't seem to grasp it.)

So then we were off to Kathy's. Her Mum turns out to be really cool with a nose stud and long red hair like Nicole Kidman. Her partner is a sculptor and there were all these incredible carvings everywhere. Like, in the corner of the lounge, there was a statue of a naked woman with ginormous breasts. Of course the guys couldn't stop gawping.

And Kathy's boobs aren't exactly pint-sized, either. She had on a skin-tight halter-neck top with no bra. I felt like a bit of a drongo in my purple number and if I could have ripped those silly bells off, honest to God, I would have.

Luckily there was a heap of food and I managed to plough my way through a whole slab of brie cheese single-handedly because no one else seemed interested. The boys skulled a can of beer each while Kathy and I had a glass of sparkling grape juice in a fancy wine-glass.

The conversation wasn't exactly riveting but thankfully Kathy's mum stayed and we managed to waffle on about what we did in the holidays or something.

So, it was a relief to get to the hall, which looked fantastic, by the way. The whole ceiling was covered in streamers – orange, blues and reds – with a huge mirror ball in the centre and yucca plants everywhere. The theme was Mexican and Mr Tafea had one of those big sombrero hats. I felt more comfortable in familiar territory.

Mike got us a glass of punch and we sat at a table near the stage. When Gemma and Zoe arrived you could tell something was wrong as soon as they walked in because instead of making their usual grand entrance they were huddled together and it looked like Gemma was crying because Zoe had her arm around her – all drama-queen like.

Anyway, Kathy went to the loo and came back with the goss. Apparently, Luke McAnally (Gemma's partner) had been refused entry on account of not being able to stand up properly and getting stroppy with Mr Hopkins, after drinking a whole bottle of wine at the Japanese restaurant that Gemma's Dad shouted them to. Ha! Served him right. I couldn't help having a grin about it, but everyone else was rushing round making a fuss and finding Gemma a seat (at the table next to us!) and looking all serious and concerned. You can imagine.

The music finally started and I had the first dance with Mike before he rushed off to the loo. It wasn't easy getting the steps right, especially in the dress, and I was starting to wish I'd paid a bit more attention to Miss Rainer during PE. Mark wasn't back in time for the next dance so I decided to take some photographs for the paper while I was waiting. (Nice shot of the drummer and also one of Mr and Mrs Hopkins who looked really sweet in matching tuxedos.) Anyway, I must have been away too long because when I got back guess who'd nicked my seat?

Little Miss feel-sorry-for-me-because-my-boyfriend-got-drunk-and-wasn't-allowed-in Scott was moving into my blind date. No prizes for guessing what happened next.

I'll spare you the gory details because it was all too humiliating. But, to cut a long story short, Gemma Scott and Mike Maxwell practically danced the night away with him all over her like a rash and her being only too happy to oblige. So embarrassing! And when it came time for the last dance I was so hanging out to leave. I don't know what Mike's intentions were about giving me a lift home but if I was going to have any dignity I needed to get in first. So I made up some story about getting a ride with a friend and, surprise, surprise, he didn't argue.

So there I was, walking home by myself. Everyone else off to the after-party at Jessie Hilton's and me walking home in the rain on my lonesome. Oh yeah, I forgot to mention that bit. It was pissing down! Can you imagine a sadder sight in the world than that?!

Well, I was heading along Ralston Street when a car slowed down beside me. At first I thought it was a stalker and my heart was going like the clappers trying to remember that stuff we learned in self-defence last year. (Is it the eyeballs or the other balls you're supposed to go for?) Anyway, I started to take off my shoes so I could make a run for it.

But then a voice said, 'Hey, what's a nice girl like you doing walking home in the rain by herself?' And I recognised the voice so I stopped – and it was Tim, that Year Twelve guy from the newspaper. He asked would I like a ride and I said where to and he said wherever I want and I said oh, yes please, that'd be great (but I hope not sounding too desperate or anything). Turned out his partner went home early because she didn't feel well and apparently, she's not exactly his partner but just a cousin and ... well, I won't bore you with ALL the details, except for the last bit.

Which is this – Tim pulled up outside my house and we talked for a bit about the newspaper story and stuff. Then I said thanks for the ride and he said that's okay and, well, when he looked at me, Jo, I went all soggy inside. Hard to explain. Sort of squirmy: my stomach felt like it was going up ten flights in the elevator or something. And I had this feeling that he wanted to kiss me but I didn't know if I was imagining it or not. It all seemed a bit surreal, especially after the fiasco with Mike Maxwell. And that's why I can't go to sleep. Because I keep seeing his face and feeling my stomach go up like in an elevator.

Hmmnnnnn...

Missing you heaps,
Issy

Dear Issy,

Do you know what I think?

I think you've had a lucky escape. That Mike Maxwell character sounds like a total moron with the personality of a school desk and the manners to match. Certainly not in the least deserving of you. I hope you got some good photos for the paper.

Take care.

Luv,

Jo

P.S. Tell me more about Tim.

Dear Jo,

Cute smile. Interesting ears. He gave me a bite of his
Jellytip ice cream at a newspaper meeting yesterday.
    Luv,
    Issy

Dear Issy,

A bite of his Jellytip??!! Wow! Sounds serious!
    Luv,
    Jo

D,
I got a letter from Issy today. She's gone all gooey over
some guy from the newspaper.

P.S. It's happened. I am turning into Hairy Maclary. And
it's not only my legs! This morning I discovered I am
growing facial hair! Dot said that's what happens when
your body weight gets low. (She also said you lose your
sex hormones. I said I didn't know I had any.)

Dear Jo,

It's me. Dad. The hospital phoned yesterday to say you had lost more weight. I am so worried. The doctor has organised a meeting at the hospital and it would be great if we could get together. Please telephone and let me know.

Luv,
Dad

Dear Mum,

Do you remember that time when our fridge broke down
– only it wasn't actually the fridge, just a blown fuse? But
we ended up getting a new one anyway.

What a laugh that was, eh.

Issy,

Have you ever had a row with your Mum and told her you hated her?

Jo,

Hell no. She'd kill me if I told her that.

Issy,

Kill you?!

Things your parents tell you:
- If the wind changes your face will stay like that.
- Eat your crusts and your hair will go curly.
- Carrots help you see in the dark.
- Only the good die young.
- Sticks and stones may break your bones but names will never hurt you.

D,

Sticks and stones may break your bones but names
will never hurt you. Yeah, right!

But some words are even sharper than swords.

Issy and I had been going to Brownies since
we were seven. And now we were both 'Sixers',
which meant that we each had a group of
younger girls to look after. Usually Issy's mum
took us to Brownies and back on a Monday night.
It was easier that way because she did a lot of
helping out and besides, Mum had Matt to look
after.

It was going to be our second ever camp and we
were really excited. The camp was at some place
near the beach and you got to stay for three nights
in bunkrooms. Friday, Saturday and Sunday. Three
of the mothers, including Issy's, stayed on to cook
and help out. We did all sorts of things at camp.
Like, we went for walks and made cards with dried
flowers and we toasted marshmallows at night
and played housie and charades and stuff. Nine-
year-old stuff. At the end of the camp Issy and I
had six new badges. We were stoked! Issy's mum
was great. She knew how to get people organised,
that's for sure. Issy said it was a pain having her
mum there but I think she really quite liked it. The
other girls thought she was cool too.

They needed two volunteers to come and

131

help clean up on Monday before we went home. That's what Mum was going to do. She arrived after breakfast. The camp helpers were all having a laugh in the kitchen and I could see Mum from the window. She'd parked the car miles down the road like she always did, even at the supermarket, because she was such a nervous driver. As soon as I saw her I got a sinking feeling. She always looked worse when I hadn't seen her for a while – with those slumped shoulders and flat hair. Her pants were all baggy and I watched her trudge up the driveway dragging her feet like blocks of concrete. Matt raced on ahead, happy as Larry. He must have been about four then.

I saw Mum arrive but I didn't rush up to meet her. Instead, I stood back and waited for her to come to me. She gave me this weak smile and a quick hug before Brown Owl shoved a broom in her hand. She looked relieved to have something to do. Poor Mum – she was never good at small talk.

A while later we were all sitting round together getting our new badges and stuff. We'd made 'thank you' cards for the helpers and we were practising a new song. Everyone was having a good time until suddenly Brown Owl appeared at the door with my brother Matt. 'This young man is in need of a mother,' she said grimly. She looked so serious that everyone stopped talking and Mum dropped her broom and raced over. Matt looked upset, like he'd been crying.

I'll never forget the look on Mum's face. Or how everyone

stared while Brown Owl explained how Matt was found wandering down the road on his own, near the railway line. Brown Owl said everything was all right now – but you could tell what she was thinking. You could tell what everyone was thinking.

I can still see the look of horror on Mum's face when she realised what'd happened. She'd obviously forgotten about Matt completely. Gone off into one of her trances. And he'd wandered off and could have been killed. Then Mum let out this groan and collapsed onto a chair.

'No harm done then,' said Brown Owl, trying to lighten things up a bit. I stayed in the circle trying to ignore everything but my face was getting hotter and hotter. I suppose I was embarrassed. (Or ashamed.) And Mum just sat there holding Matt and stroking his hair and looking about as miserable as I'd ever seen her – as if life was some puzzle she couldn't quite work out. And then she started to cry and someone went and sat with her but it wasn't me. All I wanted to do was crawl under a rock.

I can't quite remember what happened next. We had lunch and then a farewell ceremony in the garden, I think. But I remember getting in the car and looking over at Mum with her bloodshot eyes, and I just felt so angry. I couldn't help it. Why can't you be like everyone else, I thought. Why do you always have to be like this? It's not fair!

And then I said it.

'I HATE YOU.'

I didn't mean it. I really didn't. I'd never said it before but I couldn't help myself. 'I WISH YOU WERE DEAD.' It just slipped out. And I couldn't take it back. And maybe I didn't want to. But then I felt sick.

That day something inside me turned mean and hard. And there was nothing I could do to stop it. Nothing.

And it's still there now, hard as rock. Like a closed fist in my gut. And nothing I do can ever make it go away.

Except, perhaps … throwing up.

D,

We did collage with the new OT today. We sat there with magazines and scissors cutting stuff out. It was supposed to be a kind of self-portrait. Veronica said to make an image of something that had meaning for us, which was quite a fun idea and it was interesting to see what the others came up with. Like, Kara spent such a long time getting everything cut straight that she didn't get much glued on at all. (And then of course there was the inevitable hand washing routine to follow.)

Leon's portrait was very musical, with a border of black and white stripes that looked like the keyboard on a piano and lots of semi-quaver shapes in the middle. Ingrid's was lovely – very flowery and sweet. Tegan managed to find a couple of horses to focus on, surprise, surprise, and I farted around for ages before putting mine

together. In the end I did two. For the first one
I cut out two tennis racquets from an old Rebel
Sports catalogue – I stuck them in the middle of
the paper and made a background out of all sorts
of other stuff. The racquets were supposed to rep-
resent Issy and me. Then I noticed a ball of black
wool in the materials box and I had another idea.
This time I got a new piece of paper and I made a
pattern on the paper using the wool. I cut the wool
into lengths and strung it across the page and
before I knew it I'd made a spider's web.

When we got home from the Brownie camp Mum
and I kept out of each other's way. We pretended
like nothing had happened in the car. Like no one
had said anything wrong at all. Sticks and stones
may break my bones ... and all that...

I remember Mum making a special effort with
tea. We had roast chicken, which was Dad's favourite. And hokey pokey ice cream for pudding, which
was mine. Then I had a bath. But I felt bad. And
that night in bed I lay there working out how to
say sorry. There was no easy way. Sorry, Mum. I
didn't mean it. I ... Look, about that ... Maybe I'd
wait until Dad went to work.

But by then it was too late. Because when I
woke up that morning Mum was gone. She'd
taken the car and gone. Vanished. Dad thought

she'd gone to the loo in the night and stayed up for a while because she couldn't sleep. She did that sometimes. Sometimes she made tea and put the tele on at four in the morning. Except that this time she didn't make it back to bed. And she'd taken a suitcase as well.

I don't remember much about that day but I do remember Pop coming over and screaming at Dad, like it was all his fault. Dad was actually quite calm, considering. He kept saying that everything was going to be okay. Mum had taken the car and her wallet, which meant she also had her credit card. And if she was going to do anything stupid she'd hardly have taken her credit card, Dad said. It wasn't until ages after that I realised what he meant by 'anything stupid'. 'Anything stupid' meant 'do yourself in' or 'jump off a cliff'. Anything stupid meant suicide. Because that's what people like Mum did. Not that I knew that then.

She hadn't left a note, which was a good thing, according to Dad. Maybe she just needed a break. Pop didn't agree. Pop was going nuts. It was his idea to call the police.

I was so scared when the police arrived. I knew it was all my fault. I knew that Mum had left because of what I'd said to her and the police were bound to find out in the end. They'd only have to look at me to know… It'd be written all over my face. I couldn't bear it. I couldn't bear thinking about what I'd said and the look on Mum's face when I'd said it. I might as well have stabbed her with a knife. Or driven her to the edge of the cliff myself.

So I laid low, spending most of the day hiding in my bedroom and making bargains with God. Weird how I'd never thought much about God before and now I was pleading like crazy with him. 'Please God, I will keep my room tidy forever and ever if you just let Mum walk through the front door. Please God, I promise never to tease Matt ever again in my life if only … Please God, please, please make Mum come home so I can tell her I'm sorry.' But God wasn't listening because Mum didn't come back. And not only that but they never found any sign of the car, either. Not that they didn't try. Her photograph was everywhere – even on the TV.

Missing Woman

Local woman Miranda Morrison has been missing since June 18. She was driving a 1986 white Mazda Familia hatchback. Police say the 35-year-old woman suffered from depression and may have left the house in a distressed state.

There have been no reported sightings of the car and her credit card hasn't been used since her disappearance.

I was worried about the 'distressed state' bit. Did that mean she was still wearing her pyjamas?

For a while nothing much changed. It was just like Mum was in hospital again. Dad went to work each day and Mrs Jordan came over to clean the bathroom and have a tidy up. And Aunty Kay helped out sometimes. But mostly, Dad tried to carry on like everything was normal. We all did.

Pop came around as well but he was always going on at Dad in his gruff old Scottish voice. 'You should n'ya let things get so bad…' Always growling. Always arguing. Always rowing. Then one day they had a humungous argument and the next thing Pop was moving away to be near Aunty Kay. Dad said Pop was old and set in his ways. A stubborn old codger who liked to blame everyone else. Dad also told me that Pop never went to visit Mum when she was in hospital. Not even once. Didn't like that kind of thing, he said.

Our family is so not touchy feely. We usually keep our feelings to ourselves. Especially Dad. Except for that day when I came home from school and he was crying. I'd never seen Dad cry before and it was awful. He was too big to cry. Too old. And it looked all wrong – with his shoulders heaving up and down. I felt scared then. Really scared, because I knew, at that moment, how bad things were. I also knew that I could never tell Dad the truth about why Mum left. Never!

One day a police car pulled up and a man and a woman came inside our house. The woman wore a uniform. The man was in plain clothes. They asked loads of questions. Dad offered them a cup of tea and some of Mrs Jordan's shortbread. He got out the good cups and saucers from the china cabinet. They are going to find out now, I thought. This time they are definitely going to find out. And in a way I wanted them to. Except that I didn't have the guts to tell them myself.

Afterwards, the police wanted to talk with me alone. They asked weird questions, like had I ever heard Mum and Dad fighting. And did they argue a lot and had I ever seen Dad hit Mum. Of course not. (Dad never hits anyone, I said.)

They asked all the wrong questions and they left without finding out the truth.

School was the worst part, with everyone knowing. Jimmie Whaanga from Room 11 asked if we had thought of looking for Mum in the garden because last year someone went missing and they found her buried in the backyard under the blackcurrant bushes.

When Mum first left, Dad talked as though she'd be back any minute. 'Keep that drawer tidy for when your mother gets back,' he'd say. Or – 'Maybe we could borrow Mrs Jordan's caravan again when we're all together again...'

I don't know when he stopped saying stuff like that or when we stopped talking about Mum so much. I still tried to make deals with the man upstairs. Like, okay then, what about if I give all my pocket money to the Salvation Army? Huh? But time went by and Mum still hadn't returned.

And one day I realised that I hadn't written about her in my stories at school for ages. And I'd stopped saying 'Mum and Dad' like they were one person and I hadn't set her place at the table by mistake for a long time. Then I noticed her toothbrush gone, which was scary because I didn't know if she'd taken it with her or if Dad had thrown it out. I couldn't remember and I was too scared to ask.

Not thinking about it was the only way to cope.

It's funny how your memory works. Like, sometimes I lose the picture of Mum in my mind. Sometimes I can't remember the exact colour of her hair or the shape of her face. Or how tall she was. And then I panic. The only thing I remember vividly is the look on her face, in the car, after Brownie camp...

Life goes on. That's what everyone says.

Dad started playing touch rugby, which is like normal rugby except that you're not allowed to tackle. He played with the guys from work on Thursday nights. I liked Thursday nights because Mrs Jordan came over to put Matt and me to bed. I looked forward to it all day. She let us stay up late sometimes and taught us how to play cards.

She played Snap with Matt and always let him win. Then, after Matt went off to bed, we played Last Card.

She didn't always let me win but sometimes I managed it. I love cards. Later on she taught me Poker and we played with matchsticks and sometimes ten-cent pieces.

I think Mrs Jordan felt sorry for Dad. She was always saying what a good job he did and how hard it must be. She thought he deserved a night out with the boys and looking after us was the least she could do.

One night there was a phone call and Mrs Jordan came racing over to mind us kids while Dad went off to the police station. They wouldn't say what it was about but I knew it was serious because Mrs Jordan hugged him before he went and Mrs Jordan and Dad didn't normally hug. (She's not touchy feely either.)

But we had poached eggs and sausages for dinner and when Dad got back he was white as a ghost and needed a glass of Pop's whiskey (kept in the top cupboard for special occasions).

The next day at school Jimmie Whaanga told the class for news that someone's clothes had been found washed up on Castle's Beach. He had the newspaper clipping to prove it.

Police have confirmed that the
clothes found on Castle's Beach
do not belong to missing local
woman, Miranda Morrison.
Initially police had believed the
clothes might belong to the missing
woman. The clothes have now been
claimed by a local body surfer.
Police still have no clues to the
whereabouts of Mrs Morrison.

Next day – 2:30a.m. and I can't sleep.
How can anyone expect to sleep in hospital when it's
never dark or quiet? The night shift nurses seem to revel
in making as much racket as they can, especially mean old
Morag who has a very irritating humming habit, which
sounds a hundred times worse at two in the morning. I
guess you can't blame her – it must be a pig of a job at
times, tending to us loonies.

Some noises are better than others. Like Morag's
humming gets on my nerves whereas the rattle of the tea
trolley is actually quite soothing. Funny that. The best
noise of all is Leon, strumming his guitar in his room.

You have to listen hard but it's worth it. Leon could strum me to sleep any day.

Charlotte's web is spreading over the curtain rod now. Leon said the reason why spider webs don't go mouldy is because they have a special anti-bacterial quality. No wonder he's king of Trivial Pursuit. King of useless information more like.

Speaking of Leon – his mum AND dad came to visit yesterday. His mum doesn't look anything like I expected. She has white blonde hair cut in a bob and was wearing a lacy red top under a black velvet jacket. Quite the stunner, I thought. His dad, on the other hand, is geeky looking with black-rimmed glasses. They don't look like a couple at all and they don't look very comfortable in the psych ward either.

Leon and I were playing cards in the lounge when they arrived but Leon had his back to the door so it was me who saw them first – kind of hanging together in the doorway like they didn't know where to go.

When Leon heard his father's voice he dropped the whole pack of cards on the floor.

His dad looked seriously embarrassed while his mum stared straight ahead as if she was preparing for some-thing difficult. Like walking the plank perhaps.

'Can we go somewhere, Leon?'

'Sorry, Jo,' says Leon, getting up. 'Back soon.'

His parents followed him out the door without a word. That's par for the course around here: no one introduces anyone in this place. We keep our private lives separate and visitors must feel like intruders. I wonder if that's how Issy felt when she came to visit.

So, Leon went off with his folks while I played Patience.

But he was back again in half an hour looking totally miserable.

When I asked how it went he didn't answer, just grabbed the cards and started shuffling. I kept my mouth shut, figuring he was gonna crack sooner or later – which he did.

'They're back together,' he said, finally. 'He's bloody moved back in.'

'Your dad?'

'Yeah.'

'Well? That's good, isn't it?'

'No.'

'Why not?'

He shrugged. 'Because it's not going to change any-thing, is it?! Like, it's not going to change who I am and it's not going to stop them blaming each other for it.'

I wanted to ask what for but I managed to hold my tongue. It was prickly territory and I felt sorry for him.

But I could never keep my big gob shut for long. 'There's nothing wrong with being gay, you know, Leon,' I said. Then, for one horrible moment, I thought I'd got it wrong and maybe he wasn't gay after all because he looked so totally shocked.

'Sorry… I didn't mean –' I could feel my face go red.

He picked his cards up. 'You didn't mean what?' He managed to look both offended and amused at the same time. But there was a smirk leaking through like he knew how awkward I felt and was enjoying watching me squirm. And just when I was about to die from embarrassment he rescued me.

'Is it that obvious?' he said, and then grinned and we both cracked up laughing. As relieved as each other, probably.

Bad news – Francine was rushed through to the main hospital in the middle of the night. I could hear them clattering about in the corridor in the early hours.

Dear Jo,

God, I have such a sore throat. When I mentioned it to Mum she flew into some new Florence Nightingale routine. It's almost like she's waiting for an excuse to start pampering me, which is so not like her. As you know, Jo, a day off school in our house is like a once in a decade treat and only if you are struck down with something deadly or contagious or both. The exact opposite to your soft-as-butter dad!

Anyway, not this time. This time, one mention of my throat and she's out with the lemons and honey and wiping my fevered brow and booking me in for sick leave without me even asking.

It's like 'be nice to Issy' week and it doesn't take a rocket scientist to figure out why. I suspect the family knows about what happened at the dance, which means they have heard about my blind date hanging around for less than two hours before finding someone better. How humiliating. I can't stand them all feeling sorry for me and even Meredith is being half-pie decent, which is totally puke-making.

Anyway, they've been acting weird and I'm sure that's why. I just want to forget the whole thing. I mean who cares about rotten Mike Maxwell anyway. Because, like you say, I had a lucky escape.

Luv,

Issy

P.S. Oh, I forgot to tell you. When Gemma and Mike arrived at the after party there was someone waiting for them. Luke!!! He must have sobered up enough to make a return appearance. Apparently there was an ugly scene. Oh, to have been a fly on the wall, eh.

Dear Issy,

Just desserts, Issy. Just desserts. Yeah, a fly on the wall would be fun.
    Luv,
    Jo

P.S. I miss you and I wish I could leap out of bed and give you a great big hug.

Dear Jo,

Me too.

Hey, your dad phoned here the other night wanting to know if I had any news. I felt really sorry for him, Jo. He sounded worried and kind of desperate. I think you should let him visit. What harm can it do?

Luv,

Issy

Dear Issy,

Please drop it. I can't face Dad right now… and that's all there is to it.

D,

Had a good talk with Dot yesterday. I think it was
the most honest I've ever been with anyone about
throwing up (including myself). The good thing
about Dot is that she doesn't talk down to you,
which makes it easy to tell her stuff. Maybe I told
her too much. I'm so used to being secretive that
it's become like part of my nature, which is weird
because it's not the way I used to be. I've always
been more an upfront type.

Anyway, I was trying to be honest. When
I think about my binges, they've always been
at some really emotional time or when I'm not
coping. Like when Aunty Kay came I'd start out
feeling confused and then I'd get angry. I think
it was because she reminded me of Mum and
she had this new baby and stuff. And eating kind
of helped. But then, after I'd eaten so much I'd feel
disgusting and have to get rid of it. When I first
started throwing up it was only after bingeing but
then it became a habit and now I throw up after
everything. Now I don't keep anything down at all.

One of the patients in here cuts herself – I
won't say which one because that's against the
rules. But the other day she was talking about how
she feels afterwards. It sounded so familiar – the
feelings and everything. When I first started
throwing up I'd feel good afterwards. Relieved.

Emptied out. De-stressed. Now I just feel revolting and guilty.

Like I said, we all have to stay in the dining room for at least half an hour after meals and if you have to go to the loo then one of the nurses goes with you, which is pretty embarrassing when you think about it. But that half hour, for me, is like torture. It's like being denied my fix – like some druggie or something. That's what I was trying to explain to Dot.

Group Therapy Homework:

Things people do to harm themselves:
Cut, pull hair (their own), binge, starve, take drugs,
   steal stuff.

Dear Mum,

They haven't said when we're allowed ~~out~~ home yet but
I hope it's soon. Yesterday, as a special treat, we were
allowed to order our favourite meal. I chose homemade
scones with cheese melted on top, like you used to make.
Remember how you let me help with mixing the dough
and I always had the first one hot from the oven? We'd
pile the butter on thick, and jam too. Apricot jam. The
other thing I loved was apple crumble with whipped
cream and runny custard.

Dad isn't nearly as good a cook as you. When you first
left we had hot chips a lot. Dad would get them on his
way home from work and we had chips with absolutely
everything. It's better now. Dad has this little repertoire
going. Like, on Monday it's sausage casserole, on Tuesday
it's something with mince like spaghetti bolognaise or
nachos, on Wednesday it's fish pie with mashed spuds,
Thursday it's stir-fry and Friday it's macaroni cheese. In
the weekend it's just whatever's around.

I haven't had hot chips in months.

They don't do them here.

Take care,
Jo

P.S. I was reading some stuff about spiders. Apparently the spider lays her eggs in autumn, wraps them in a silk bag and then gets ready to die. The interesting thing is, after laying the eggs she is so exhausted that she simply can't carry on, which is why you don't see many spiders about in winter.

I was wondering, Mum. Was that how you felt after having Matt?

Fishing

I fish around the clear blue lake
Watching. Waiting.
In the silence I hear a jump.
A fish, a fish, a fish, I cry!
With all that screaming, I look around.
The fish has gone.
Perhaps he drowned.

By Johanna Morrison – aged 8

The Fat Cat

I have a new cat
It sits on the mat
It is very, very fat
Because it eats lots of pies.
I'm going to be sad when it dies.
Because it has bad cholesterol
From all the pies.

By Johanna Morrison – aged 10

D,

In group therapy the other day Caroline was telling
us about this great-aunty of hers who'd never touched
alcohol all her life until she had some Christmas cake
with sherry in it when she was seventy-eight years old.
And the sherry must have triggered something off inside
because after that she became an alcoholic. Leon didn't
believe her. He said that sounded like a load of bollocks
and who ever heard of someone becoming an alcoholic
after eating Christmas cake. But Veronica said don't scoff
because addictions can be very strange things. She said
they're just like allergies in a way and sometimes people
get addicted to things they're allergic to. Like, for example,
someone with a wheat allergy could develop a craving for
pasta.

We talked about it for a while. How people get addicted to things like cigarettes and even numbers and tidy bedrooms and throwing up.

When you think about it, the world must be full of addicted people. The question is, how come only some of us end up in mental institutions?

D,

Solitary confinement again. Bed rest. No privileges. No showering. Nothing to read and no one to talk to because Dot's been away all week. I miss her when she's off work. She's such a hoot and the only one here with any sense of humour. She reminds me of Mrs Jordan (a bit plumper but just as kind). Like, the other day she brought me a tin of homemade fudge. If only I could eat it… If only the smell of it didn't turn my stomach…

Anyway …

Last night I had this dream about Charlotte. She had grown huge and was stalking across me with big hairy legs (which, incidentally, were even worse than mine). Right across my face until I woke up screaming. The bedclothes were off and I lay there shivering and feeling sorry for myself. I didn't have the energy to cover myself up so I just lay there. Pathetic, huh?!

Leon has gone home for a few days and I'm really worried about him. He's got very quiet and seems more confused than ever. Plus, he gets this weird kind of look in his eyes sometimes. I think he feels responsible for his mum and dad's break-up. Like, if he were the perfect son it'd all be okay. Yeah, right! It really does my head in sometimes.

From what I can work out, his mum is totally in charge and his dad just follows along to keep the peace. They blame each other for Leon being in hospital. It's like they think being gay is somebody's fault. Leon was dreading going home. I think now that they've moved back together he feels responsible for that as well: as if they think that now they're going to all live happily ever after, their son won't have to be gay any more. Bollocks!

I wonder sometimes if feeling sad is contagious. If it is, then places like this must only make matters worse. For example, since I've been in here my exercise regime has gone completely to pot. And exercise is supposed to be good for you. Isn't it? They can't have it both ways.

I have become such a slug. I can't remember the last time I did some sneaky press ups and these days I can't even be bothered to read. I used to love reading. Getting lost in a book was, like, the best thing in the world... Tamora Pierce and Sheryl Jordan were my favourite authors. But these days I can't concentrate on anything longer than a page. This letter has taken me all morning to write but who cares. I've got nothing better to do.

D,

It's the middle of the night and I can't sleep because the gap in these curtains is irritating the hell out of me. Everything irritates me these days. It's like having constant heat rash and I want to scratch myself raw. In fact, writing is the only thing that keeps me sane.

Sometimes I feel like I'm down a black hole. Or I'm in that water with the eels – going round and round, getting all tangled in the weed. I lay here last night looking at the painting and trying to will myself into it. It was like I wanted to be right there in that sea with the waves thrashing and the undertow dragging me down. They say drowning is a nice way to go. But how do people know stuff like that? Maybe they just make it up. There was a story in the *Woman's Weekly* about a baby drowning in an inch of bath water. Sometimes I think you don't need any water to drown.

I haven't had a letter in ages. They're keeping them from me until I start eating again. Maybe I could drink something. Maybe I'll have some yoghurt. Maybe … But my mouth is cracking at the sides and I've got ulcers on my tongue. I am ugly. Ugly. Ugly.

Dear Jo,

School is so, so, so, so boring just now. Mr Tafea is making
us memorise formulas for Science and for History we are
studying Adolf Hitler, except that I'm not going to do my
essay because I think that man's had far too much pub-
licity already. I think it would be better to study someone
who's made a positive contribution to world history like
Gandhi or Martin Luther King, Jr. or even Elvis Presley.
Hey, at least he brought some joy into the world. What
is it with writing essays about warmongers? Seems like
you get to do all the good people at primary school and
then when you get to high school they hit you with the
monsters.

My career as a photographer took a major blow yesterday when we tried to publish the formal photographs and
got a row of ghosts instead. Complete balls up.

So the newspaper people now think I'm a total moron.

Dear Issy,

No one thinks you are a moron. You are the sweetest
smartest girl on the planet and don't let anyone tell you
any different.

   Jo

P.S. I know why they make us study Hitler. It's because he
was so evil and wicked and they think if we learn about
why he was like that then all that evil won't happen again.
But some people are born evil and that's that. Some people
only ever think about themselves. Some people have absolutely no feeling for others...
P.P.S. Have you run into that Tim guy again lately?

Dear Jo,

Thanks for that completely biased summary of my personality.

   Yes, I have run into Tim again. Twice! But I've decided
to steer clear because every time I see him I turn into a
complete drongo. Honestly, I don't know what gets into me.

   Remember how I told you about that elevator thing
I have going in my tummy? Well, that feeling has now
evolved into something more serious: with my mind going
completely blank, my voice coming out all screwy and

my brain losing the ability to form sentences.

It's a bit like stage fright and instead of wowing him with warm and witty conversation I go 'Duh, uh, umm yeah.' Then I giggle and go bright red. Might as well dye my hair blonde and be done with it.

All my love,
Issy

P.S. I don't agree about the 'evil' thing because I don't think anyone's born evil. It's society that makes them like that.

Dear Issy,

Sorry, I have no advice on the 'boy' front. The only male contact I've had for the past couple of months has been Leon and he doesn't really count in that respect.

P.S. Please don't go blonde on me – you are absolutely not dizzy enough to pull it off.

Dear Jo,

Breaking news.

The other night Kate shouted me to a movie. Yes, I know, I was as shocked as you. (I think it was a sympathy thing.) Anyway, it was Kate's treat and she chose this movie called *River Queen*, because it's a New Zealand film and there was all this controversy and also because she knew someone who worked on the set as a stand-in or something.

Well, about three-quarters of the way through, I notice this familiar head shape two rows in front. (Hey, I'd recognise those ears anywhere.) It's Tim. Luckily the movie is nearly over, because now I can't concentrate. Not trusting myself to carry out a casual conversation I decide to evacuate my seat asap, which would have worked out fine if it hadn't been for Kate wanting to sit through to the bitter end so she can see her friend's name come up on the credits.

Of course, this time he sees me and he gets this big dopey look on his face. We say hello, and I go through my 'dah, um, er bright red face' routine again. But then he introduces me to this girl called Geraldine. I hadn't noticed anyone with him before that and suddenly I feel like such an idiot.

And to make matters worse Kate starts going on about how she reckons he fancies me and I know she's only saying it because she thinks that's what I want to hear, but I don't. Because what I want to do is scream and say, oh, yeah, right, maybe that's why he has someone called Geraldine strapped to his arm!

Advertisement on chemist shop window:

D,

They are going to put me on a potassium drip. I will be
hooked up to a heart monitor and have my temperature
taken every hour.

D,

Aunty Kay said that when I was a kid I was built like a
pencil but now I was starting to get curves – like Mum.
That's what started me off – a silly thing like that.

I can remember the day I started my diet. It was Saturday, November the sixteenth.

I used to keep my old exercise books from school in a
box under the bed. So I found one that was only half full
and started writing down goals. First up, I promised to
write down everything I ate for the next two weeks. It felt
good to have a plan and be in charge for once.

The next day I ate absolutely nothing all day except
for one piece of fish (without the batter) and seven and a
half chips. (No kidding – that's what I wrote – 'seven and
a half' chips!) I recorded every single thing I ate (every sip
and every crumb).

Example:
Monday – One slice toast with Marmite. One sausage.
Eight glasses of water.
Tuesday – One pottle mixed berry yoghurt.

Wednesday – Two sausage rolls and half a Weetbix.

It was easier than I thought. I could go without eating for a whole day if I tried. Nothing to it! In fact, if I stayed busy and away from food it was a doddle. Will power and water! That's all you need. And I had truckloads of both. Missing breakfast was a breeze because Dad was too busy to notice and he doesn't eat breakfast anyway. I felt guilty turfing out the lunch he made me, but it was all for a good cause.

If Dad worked late he left dinner in the fridge for Matt and me to heat in the microwave. Sometimes I ate the vegies but usually I biffed the whole lot in the compost heap, under the grass clippings, so he wouldn't find out.

Not eating isn't nearly as hard as you think. You go through the hunger and out the other side. Endure, ignore and eventually it goes away. Eventually. Usually. (Well, mostly!)

Except that every now and then hunger arrived like a great huge bear demanding to be let in. Bang! Bang! Bang! Growling in fury and making a fist in my belly. Sometimes I gave in to it, scoffing everything in sight – stuffing it down in a frenzy. Cold pies, raw bacon, stale bread. Whatever was on hand. The more revolting the better, because eating is disgusting. I am disgusting. Puking into the rubbish bin is disgusting, too. But not as disgusting as not puking. Not as disgusting as having curves, like Mum. I got back on track fast, recording everything in my notebook:

'Tomorrow not one morsel of food will pass my lips. Tomorrow I will run ten kilometres without stopping. Tomorrow …'

Tomorrow I go on the potassium drip.

Dear Jo,

Guess what?! Geraldine is his sister. Isn't that a coincidence?! Both of us at the movies with our sisters!! I only found out yesterday. Feel so much better now.

He says, 'Do you like the movies?'

I say, 'Sometimes.'

He says, 'I only went because my sister shouted?!'

I say, 'Really? Me too!'

(Fancy that, eh!)

Luv,
Issy

Group Therapy Homework:

I feel powerful when … I am hungry
My best asset is … My will power

Dear Mr Morrison,

As discussed over the phone we have placed your daughter Johanna on a potassium drip. We would also like to recommend a family approach. In our experience psychotherapy works well in combination with family therapy. Please phone or call and we'll make an appointment to discuss further treatment.

Yours sincerely,

Neville Fraser (Dr)

Noticeboard:

> OT – This week we'll be continuing with collage.

D,

We had this discussion about Francine in group today. If Veronica was trying to scare the pants off us … well, I guess it worked. They say she is going to die soon because her organs are failing.

They're always on about people dying from anorexia but you don't believe it. Not really. I mean, how can anyone die from being too skinny?!

One night, at home, I ate a whole loaf of cheese and onion bread. I didn't mean to – I just started picking at the cheese and before I knew it I'd scoffed the lot. That's how it happened. I'd start off small and lose control. Then I'd get the hiccups and vomit in the toilet.

The next morning I felt like crap. I was sick and tired of being like this. It was such a pathetic way to be. Then I had an idea. I knew what I had to do. It's weird when I think about it now, but back then it seemed like the perfect solution.

All I needed was scissors.

And the only scissors I could find were the ones Dad used to cut his toenails. They'd have to do. I started on my fringe, slicing my way from left to right – chomp, chomp, chomp, the more uneven the better. Then I just went for it until all my hair was scissored up. In the end I was chopping it down to the scalp – slicing in from different angles. I don't know what came over me but it felt right. It looked dreadful but I felt strangely satisfied. It was like I deserved it.

But … oh, my God! What a mess. I must have looked like a demented witch and when Dad came home my hair was all over the kitchen floor.

Dear Jo,

Remember the 40 Hour Famine? Remember how we got sponsored and stayed the night in the scout hall? Can you believe that was a whole year ago? Mrs Hopkins has been asking for volunteers again but I said, no thanks, I'd rather walk a mile on hot coals than go without food for that long!!

Issy

D,

The 40 Hour Famine was when Issy and I had our fight. Well, it wasn't a fight exactly but it was a pretty bad argument because we ended up not talking to each other for three days, which is the most time we have ever not spoken for, apart from lately, that is. These days we write instead.

Anyway, Mrs Hopkins organised it through school and you had to get sponsors who paid you fifty cents an hour for not eating. All the money went to the starving people in Africa. Good idea, huh? Awesome. In fact, I reckon we should do it more often. We should have regular five-day famines to make up for having so much to eat when most of the world has nothing. Or maybe we should starve ourselves every Friday and donate the proceeds. Last year I raised $48.60.

Anyway, the famine is great. You get to chill out and you're not expected to do anything except not eat, which is cruisy. People bring along videos and there's a pool table and stuff. Mostly Issy and I lie about reading and playing cards, which isn't hard work at all. In fact, it's cool having an excuse to not eat.

But Issy is hopeless and after just two hours without food she is ready to pass out. 'It's my low blood sugar problem, Jo,' she reckons. More like her low will power problem, I reckon. Issy cheats. The rule is you're allowed one barley sugar every hour so I give her my rations but still it's not enough because (to delay the onset of malnutrition), she sneaks in a packet of Pineapple Lumps, two boxes of Jaffas, and a king-size Grainwaves. And I think it pisses her off that I won't join in with the Pineapple Lumps. 'Come on, Jo. No one's gonna know. Just a few lollies. And since when did you become such a goody two shoes?' But it's not about other people knowing, is it? That's not the point. YOU know! And that's what counts.

Anyway, I must be a stubborn cow because I don't stop after forty hours like the others. They have this big countdown when the time's up – 5, 4, 3, 2, 1!!!, like New Year's Eve. And everyone starts cheering and hugging and putting in their pizza orders. But pizza is the last thing I feel like. Big, fat, globby pizza?! No thank you. What about McDonald's? says Issy. Nah! Not for me.

That's when Issy gets fed up and we have our argument, with her saying I am weird and nutty and vain and what the heck's got into me these days and me saying she's got no will power and anyway she's just jealous. So I go home and she stays for pizza and we don't speak for three days.

They are the worst three days ever, which is why I decide to keep my eating plan a secret – basically so Issy and I can be friends again with-out her thinking I'm really weird or being jealous because I'm losing weight.

It's hard though. I have to work things so she won't know. Like, if I'm over at her place and her mum asks me to stay for dinner then I have to make up some excuse like I've already eaten or I've got a tummy bug or Dad said I have to come home for dinner because he's gone to a lot of trouble. I get good at making excuses. And if I absolutely can't get out of eating then I throw up. You have to do it straight after, before the food gets digested. The trick is this – run a tap so no one hears, use the toilet spray and suck on Tic Tacs so your breath doesn't smell.

Dear Issy,

I thought we weren't going to mention that famine...

Dear Jo,

Okay then, we won't.

I wish you could meet Tim. He has this cute little turned up bit on the end of his nose like a ski jump and he has a kind of bouncy walk. Not too bouncy though. Not like a nerd or anything – well, not quite.

We are onto Shakespeare in English now. *Romeo and Juliet*. Romeo, Romeo, wherefor art thou … Miss Haddock got Danny Snell to read Romeo and he's in full flight when suddenly he cracks a high. How embarrassing – I am so glad that voice thing doesn't happen to us. I would be mortified to crack a high in front of everyone. Wouldn't you?

No more news. Sorry.

Luv,

Issy

P.S. Oh, except Pavlova went missing last week and we found her locked inside Mr Allcock's shed. Mum reckons he shut her in deliberately but, as you know, my mum is sometimes inclined to paranoia.

D,

We were talking about disguises the other day. You know, about the masks people wear. Veronica's theory is that when people get a mental disorder it's because they're not being honest about who they really are – like, sometimes who they are is different from who they're pretending to be. And the wider the gap, the more unwell they become.

Group therapy is supposed to help peel back the layers and find the real authentic person inside, which is why you have to be 100% honest about stuff. Kind of like when you take up the carpet in your house and underneath are the most amazing rimu floorboards!! Which sounds like a good plan, except for, well, what happens if you peel back the carpet and instead of finding a nice rimu floor underneath there's only chipboard?!! What then?! Do you get to put the carpet back or what? Because if the person is mean and rotten inside then maybe they need their disguise and, in that case, a few inches of shagpile to cover up the mess might be a good idea.

Veronica didn't think so. She said we are all unique and special in our own way. Hmmnnn … I bet she is trained to say that.

Yesterday we made candles with the OT lady. I decided on a Christmas theme because I love Christmas and, even though it's commercial and corny, every time I hear that song 'Little Drummer Boy' I just want to burst into tears. (Christmas is all about pretending though, eh. Like, for example, did you know that during World War One they used to have a break from fighting on Christmas Day and sometimes the enemies would even have Christmas dinner together. Only, then they'd go back to killing each other on Boxing Day. Can't remember where I heard that but I'm pretty sure it's true.)

The OT showed me this technique where you thread beads onto fine wire and then wrap the wire around the candle. Looks good.

Dad's boss at work gave us a Christmas tree last year.

It was left over from the ones at the garage – just a straggly old branch really. Mrs Jordan came to help decorate it. She'd made three bowls of popcorn that we threaded with cotton to go round the tree. It took ages but was loads of fun and we ate heaps of the popcorn.

Mum hated Christmas. She used to say how she wished she could skip December altogether. A lot of fuss about nothing, she thought.

I nearly told Mrs Jordan that night. I nearly told her about what I'd said to Mum the night before she left. I had it all worked out in my head and I had her answer all worked out as well. (She was going to say, 'Oh, that's nothing, Jo. I've said that to my own mother millions of times. Who hasn't?') I so needed to hear that. That would have been the best Christmas present, hearing someone say that. But then Matt came in wanting his shoelace tied and the phone went and … Well, by then I'd chickened out again.

So I didn't tell anyone. Still haven't. Not even Veronica, who I am expected to discuss my most intimate secrets with. Not even when she needles me about why I cut my hair.

It was cutting my hair that put me in this place to start with. Dad went nuts when he saw it. Flipped out completely. And that's when I started seeing Miss Hughes. I had a standing appointment in her office twice a week. Not that it achieved much. In fact, for the first couple of weeks I said bugger all, just let her prattle on about death and grief and stuff. There was no point in arguing because she'd already decided what my problem was and what we were going to do about it. In fact, she thought she had me all worked out. In her opinion, the best way to deal with things was to start being realistic about Mum's disappearance.

'It's been six years now, Jo,' she told me (as if I didn't know). 'And maybe you need to think about the possibility of not seeing your mum again.' She made it sound so easy. But I couldn't do it. Because if Mum was dead, then it was all because of me. Me and my big gob!

Dear Jo,

Dad really wants to see you, Sis. Me too.

    Love,

    Matt

P.S. I made nachos this week but they were too hard to wrap so I had to eat them myself. We used extra-hot chilli beans!! Yuck!

Baked beans

The musical fruit

The more you eat

The more you toot!!

Martin Wainwright farted all afternoon.

P.P.S. Please find enclosed my latest fossil. Dad reckons it could be a moa's tooth. You can keep it as a lucky charm if you like.

D,

In group therapy Veronica asked me something that fair took my breath away. We'd been having this discussion about responsibility when, out of the blue, she turned the focus on me. (That's how she operates. She'll leave you alone for ages, then wham! It's full-on interrogation.) In front of everyone, she asked if I blamed myself for Mum leaving.

Does a bear shit in the woods? I thought (which is one of Dad's favourite sayings). But I didn't say that. First, because it's not the kind of thing you say to Veronica and second, because I've never told anyone the truth before and I wasn't about to spill my guts in front of the likes of Caroline and Kara.

But she made me think.

She didn't wait for an answer. She just bowled on with another of her theories.

'It's very common,' she said, looking around the group.

What is? I thought. Telling your mother you wished she were dead and then waking up to discover she'd taken you up on it? Yeah, right. I bet that's happened to loads of people.

'Blaming yourself,' said Veronica, like she was reading my mind, 'is a natural reaction. When parents leave (as in scarper, die, or get divorced), it's common for kids to blame themselves. It happens a lot. And sometimes our feelings get out of control. And sometimes eating disorders develop as a way to control these feelings.'

Seems like she had it all sussed. She liked to talk about 'our' feelings as though it applied to her as well.

I shrugged and tried to look like I wasn't sure what she was on about. But inside, my heart was going thump, thump, thump because she'd hit a nerve. I could see she was trying to be helpful and I could see she might even have a point. But I couldn't bring myself to admit she was right. The truth was, I couldn't bear the thought

176

of anyone else knowing. I'd been working on my defence system for so long that I wasn't about to let down my guard. Well, not here, anyway.

She seemed to take the hint and carried on about a bunch of other stuff, including the fact that mental illness is sometimes inherited. Great! I felt myself go red as a beetroot when she said that because I could tell she was meaning me.

'But that doesn't mean you're stuck with it,' she said, as if she were talking about a bad case of acne. 'Mental illness, just like physical illness, can be treated. And, with the right treatment, it can also be overcome.'

Then she prattled on about how we shouldn't take responsibility for things beyond our control. And then she turned the spotlight on me again.

'You're a tough cookie, Jo,' she said, only this time I knew she was right. That's what hacked me off most. I *was* a tough cookie. At least I used to be.

D,

It's raining outside. Pissing down, in fact. And it's getting colder too. There was a frost last week. Normally I love frosts. Dad used to tell cute stories about Jack Frost. I knew they weren't true but it was nice to pretend. In the winter, it was my job to get the ice off his car windscreen in the morning. You had to get the water temperature just right because if you used cold water it froze again and if the water was too hot the windscreen could crack.

Last winter dad bought me 'toe socks' from the Two Dollar Shop. Two dollars for a pair of socks! Far out! He thought he'd done so well but they were actually the most uncomfortable things to wear. My toes felt itchy and bunched up inside them. I didn't tell Dad that.

Hey, I can see Veronica from up here. She's getting out of her car. Nice coat. Bet it's new. I can't remember the last time I had something new to wear. Maybe it was the toe socks. Trouble is, I feel fat in everything I put on. Even my toes feel fat these days.

Later:
Dot started back today. It was good to see her again and I have to say she's looking better. Her hair is cut differently, softer round her face and she's had streaks put through it. She's been up north visiting her daughter, Leah. I feel really sorry for Leah because I keep trying to put myself in her shoes and I've decided I don't know what I'd do if I found out Dad was cheating on Mum. On the one hand you'd want your mother to know the truth and on the other hand you'd be thinking how devastated she'd be when she found out and how you shouldn't be the one to tell her. Also, you might be hoping it'd all kind of fizzle

out so maybe she'd never have to know.

One thing I've learned is – you should never tell your mother bad things because you never know how she will react.

P.S. Leon and Tegan had a wicked argument today. Tegan was talking about the way her dad treats her mum and how he doesn't understand anything about horses and how difficult things are for her mum and everything. Then suddenly Leon flies off the handle. He says how come it's always the man's fault and why do males get blamed for everything, like when something goes wrong in a marriage for example. He was getting so fired up about it, I think he must have been talking about his own mum and dad.

Dear Jo,

Got my maths paper back this afternoon. 43%!!! My worst mark ever. Bummed out in algebra. My brain turned to slush. Hope I get to do a resit before Mum finds out or she'll blow her top! (Apply yourself, Isabelle. Extend that lazy mind of yours, girl.)

Had mufti day yesterday to raise money for the new gymnasium. Tim wore three-quarter pants with long socks and looked (gulp!) like he was auditioning for *The Sound of Music*!!! Hmmmnnn … What do you think?

    Luv,

    Issy

Dear Issy,

Three-quarter pants with long socks, huh? Hmmnnn … let's see. Sometimes you have to put these things in perspective. For example, if you compare it with world hunger or suicide bombers I'd say it wasn't that important. But if you were thinking of forming some sort of relationship with the guy then you might have to seriously reconsider!! Especially when you couple it with his Jellytip fetish.

Jo,
I never said he had a Jellytip fetish!!!

Issy,
Sorry. Just teasing.

DEATH NOTICES

Colson, Francine. — On 7 July, 2005, as a result of anorexia, aged 28 years. Loved daughter of Alice and Bill Colson. Loved sister of Bernadette, Angeline, Thomas, Phillip and Andrew. Loved grand daughter of Harrison and the late Eileen, also cherished grand daughter of Ted and Dorrie Parks. 'Forever in our hearts.'

A service for Francine will be held in the Church of the Holy Name on Thursday. In lieu of flowers, donations to the Eating Disorders Association would be appreciated and may be left at the service.

Hey…

Even when you know someone is dying it's still a shock when it happens, especially when the person is just 28. You just can't believe you won't see them again. Ever. Ever. Ever. Ever. Ever. Ever. Ever. Ever. And even if you say 'ever' a million times it's still not enough. And even if you didn't see them a lot in the first place it's still a hard thing to get your head around. Not existing. Here, then not here. Vanished. Disappeared. Gone. Gone. Gone. Forever and ever and ever…

There was a photograph of Francine in the newspaper. At first I thought they had the wrong person. Like, I thought the paper had made some dreadful mistake and put in this photo of some movie star or something.

God, how embarrassing, I thought. Because the Francine in the paper looked like Catherine Zeta Jones in the *Woman's Weekly*. She had this bouncy black hair and well, she looked amazing.

Veronica said the photograph was taken five years ago, before she got sick. I couldn't believe it. It was like Francine had become a completely different person and it made me feel ill just thinking about it. So what happened? How did that lovely Francine in the paper end up dead in hospital? How??!!!

No one here knew the 'other' Francine. We all

presumed she'd come from some weird place. Like maybe her parents were religious fanatics or druggies or heavy metallers or something. Except that 'Alice and Bill Colson' sound like regular people and the Church of the Holy Name doesn't sound too much like a religious cult.

In the end we decided not to go to the funeral. It was Caroline's idea to hold a memorial service of our own.

The idea seemed to catch on. Leon said he'd play his guitar and I asked if it'd be okay to read something. Before the service I went for a walk around the hospital grounds. My legs felt weak and shaky. Hard to believe what an inside person I've become especially when I used to be such a tomboy. The air felt cold between my teeth like I'd been sucking on ice and I shivered so much my bones felt like an old rattly skeleton.

In Cutler Street Dad had a glasshouse where he grew tomatoes. When they got to a certain point he'd take the plants out to 'harden them up' outside. Well, that's what I felt like – one of those plants. Like I needed a few days in the sun to harden up.

I folded my arms to keep warm and sat down on the park bench to think about what I was going to read. I'd never spoken at a memorial service before.

So where do you start and what should you say?

Dear Francine,
I don't know you very well at all but ...

Dear Francine,
What happened?

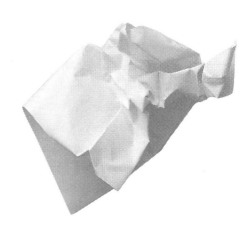

Dear Francine,

We only met a couple of times but I've read your poems
and I've seen you round the place. It's hard to imagine you
gone. I mean, it's really hard to believe.

When I look at your photograph I want to cry. I was
thinking ... maybe the rest of us should make a pledge.
Maybe we should promise ourselves to get well for you.
Because then your dying won't be for nothing. And maybe
your parents won't be so sad if they know that.

Anyway, I'd like to say – rest in peace, Francine Colson.

It doesn't say everything but it'll have to do.

This is what happened at the service. Caroline made a kind of altar on the sideboard in the 'common room'. She knew Francine best and besides, she is always happy taking charge. We lined up our candles in a row behind a photograph of the Francine we knew (white face, black clothes etc.). Veronica pinned some poetry onto a corkboard.

'Let me be weightless and airy and light – and maybe I'll find peace tonight...' (Strangely, now that she is dead, her words make a weird kind of sense.)

Veronica said a prayer. Then she told us some stuff about Francine's life. Like she was born in Sydney and came to New Zealand when she was three and she was a good netball player and she liked acting and she'd even been deputy head girl at her school. Deputy head girl?! It was hard to get your head around.

She made Francine's life into a kind of story, which I guess, when you think about it, is what our lives are. Such a sad ending though. Veronica didn't actually talk about the way she died. She didn't have to. It hung over us all like a shadow.

Leon played 'Knocking on Heaven's Door' by Bob Dylan, with hardly any clunkers. His voice is amazing. Then he blew us away by singing a song he'd written himself. It was all about making your own kind of music and being true to yourself and it made me want to cry because Leon looked like one of those old school folk singers and I felt so proud of him and it was like I had a golf ball jammed in my throat the whole way through.

When it came time to read my letter I was shaking like a leaf. I got to the bit about Francine's parents and I lost the plot. God knows what I sounded like.

After my letter Ingrid read a poem but she dropped the book halfway through and couldn't find her place so she had to sit back down. Kara didn't say anything. She just sat there with her feet in a straight line chewing her fingernails. And Pip did much the same.

When it was over, Caroline passed around a bowl of black grapes because apparently black grapes were about the only thing Francine ever ate. So we put them in our mouths and went through the usual tortuous process of swallowing. Mine sat like lead in my stomach. Kara peeled the skin off hers and nibbled. It was all so frustrating to watch and that's when I had this experience. I don't know how to describe it. It was like looking down on myself – sort of detached. It didn't last long but for one brief moment it was like I could see things differently and it was scary because I could see how I must look to other people. How we all must look. Like, imagine if someone dropped in from another planet. And there we all were – scared to eat. It hit me like a slap in the face. Scared to eat. WHY???!!! How come? How bloody come? At that moment life seemed completely bizarre.

And then I just felt shattered. And exhausted. And sick to death of everything. Like I'd just been run over by a ten ton truck.

A contract with myself

I, Johanna Margaret Morrison, do solemnly swear on all that is precious to me, that I really, really want to get well again.

My goal is to make 50 kilos. I realise it's going to be hard work but I know it's for my own good. I can't go on like this and I don't want to end up like Francine. I am going to do everything I possibly can to get well, which includes doing what the nurses tell me and not cheating or chucking up when no one's looking.

I will also keep a food diary and get back in contact with Dad.

Yours faithfully,
Johanna Morrison

D,

I've just had a long talk with Veronica and told
her there are some things I have to deal with.
She didn't take much notice at first until I said I
wanted to see Dad and then she started asking
questions. Boy, did she ask some questions! I got
scared then but when I showed her my food diary
she seemed to believe that I really am trying. The
scary thing is that no one else can help. Not even
Veronica – because when it comes down to it, I'm
on my own.

Being on your own is frightening. Knowing you
are in charge of your own destiny is scary. But I
guess it's good as well. Veronica says we can help
each other out but in the end we have to make our
own decisions. It's called 'growing up'.

I guess that is true for Mum as well.

Anyway, I know Veronica's a therapist and all
that but sometimes I'd really like to talk to her
as a friend. I'd like to tell her about my letters to
Mum and stuff but I don't want her giving me
instructions. I don't want to be one of her case
studies and I don't want to be analysed. Also, I
don't want her to panic – I'm worried she'll think
I'm nuts.

She says she'll try to organise a family conference, which makes me absolutely petrified.

Dear Mr Morrison,

In consultation with our group therapist, Veronica Brown, we would like to schedule a meeting with you and your daughter Johanna. We feel she has reached a point where progress may be made. There are obviously family issues that need addressing and the hospital environment will provide a neutral forum.

Please phone me at the above number to schedule an appointment time.

Yours faithfully,

Neville Fraser (Dr)

Dear Issy,

Things have been pretty dreadful lately. Do you remember that girl I told you about, the one in the wheelchair, who wore black lipstick?

Well, she died! I know, I can't believe it, either. It's terrible and everyone's so upset even though none of us really knew her. You might have seen the death notice in the paper. There was a photograph and she looked like Catherine Zeta Jones in the *Woman's Weekly*, except that in real life she didn't look like that at all, which is the scary part. It is the weirdest feeling knowing she's gone. We had a memorial service where we read poems and said prayers and stuff.

But the thing is, it's given me a scare and now I've decided I've got to work hard at getting out of here. From now on I'm going to concentrate on getting well because if I stay in hospital I might end up in a wheelchair like Francine and you might be saying poems at my funeral and eating black grapes. Sorry to prattle on.

I hope everything is going well at school.

Lots of luv,

Jo

D,

Looking out at the stars settles the mind and calms the spirit. I read that in a book and actually I think it's true. You should try it some time. The stars help you put things in perspective, especially when you are on the verge of losing it.

The thing is, those stars are so far away that it's hard to tell how big they are, or how important. And I guess that's the whole point. Because, in the end, what's important is up to us. When you look at the stars like that you realise how insignificant we all are. I mean, there are hundreds of galaxies out there and, in the grand scheme of things, we are smaller and about as trivial as the teeny weeniest grain of beach sand. I used to think that was depressing. But being insignificant can be quite comforting – liberating, even. Well, that's what I think. Because, if I am so insignificant, then what I do or say isn't likely to be seriously important. Which is great!

And so I'm standing in my bedroom thinking about all this (with the light off so I can see the stars) and then it hits me like a meteor. Don't ask me to explain what exactly, because I can't. It's just that suddenly I feel like I understand something new and I don't feel so trapped any more. Maybe I don't have to stay here.

It's all about choice, see. We make our choices on the basis of who we are. And we all make different choices. And it's these choices that shape our lives. And suddenly I can see that goes for Mum too.

Okay, I know she wasn't well but she still had a choice. Like, she could have asked for help or she could have told me to pull my head in or she could have taken herself back to hospital.

I've never actually felt that way before. Like I actually have a choice.

And now, when I look out at the starry sky, even though it's from behind a wad of double glazing, I have this warm feeling. Like something's melting inside.

Dear Jo,

Don't you dare have me reading poems at your memorial service. If you die on me I'll never forgive you!!! Never. Ever. Ever. Ever. Ever. Ever.

D,

Monday – half a plate of porridge, 1 quarter toast, three bites of omelette and two slices of tomato.

Unfortunately I throw it all back up because today is the day I am going to tell Dad the truth about why Mum left.

I put on the blue jumper with the Levis jeans and the white belt. My hair isn't looking great so Dot helps me tie it back. She does a French braid, which is difficult because due to my recent hair hacking, some bits are longer than others. I really need to get a proper haircut.

Dot is such a sweetie. She even brought in some make-up and helped me put on mascara and lipstick, which I ended up rubbing off because I looked like a clown. I really don't understand make-up. (Don't think it was Mum's strong point, either.)

Anyway ... when we get into the room I notice that Veronica is dressed up and looking official, which is slightly off-putting. She has a file on her knee with 'confidential' on the front! I try and take my mind off myself by glancing casually around the room. I notice there's a painting on the wall similar to the one in my room, only in this one the lighthouse is in the distance and the waves are crashing about the rocks. It's like the same scene from a different perspective.

On the filing cabinet beside Professor Plaque's desk there's a family photograph and beside the photograph is a framed poem. The red words leap out from their black background.

And the poem goes:

Grant me the serenity to accept the things I cannot change,
The courage to change the things I can,
And the wisdom to know the difference.

A shudder passes through me because the same poem is on Mum's dressing table. I've seen it a million times but I've never read the words – not properly. But they are beautiful so I read them again. And it calms me down. Then I hear Dad's cough and the next thing Veronica's patting my hand, which makes me feel about five years old. And Professor Plaque is telling Dad to 'make himself at home' and now it's all on and suddenly I'm not so sure I'm ready for this yet. Because here we all are – Dad, Matt and me. I didn't know Matt was coming. And I know it's only been a few weeks but he looks taller and his hair's grown long and well, this is all just so weird.

Dot rushes up to get Matt a seat because there aren't enough and now we're sitting in a semi-circle with me directly opposite Dad. I feel like I'm on display and I'm so nervous that when I try to smile my dry lips get stuck on my top teeth and won't come back down.

Dad looks smaller than I remember, like he's shrunk. And older. His jumper is matted like when you put the machine on a hot wash by mistake. He's always been hopeless with washing, which makes me feel guilty and want to cry.

I feel confused. Like part of me wants to race up and put my arms round them both and the other part wants to run and hide. Professor Plaque is prattling on about something but I can't concentrate. I feel itchy and hot and my breathing is going wonky.

Now Dot's going all blurry and there's not enough air in this room ... plus I need water ... plus I ...

I get up and kind of stumble backwards, knowing I'm going to ruin the meeting but also knowing I have to get out of here. I've duffed it.

'Sorry,' I say. And they're all looking at me, like 'Pardon?'

'Sorry, but I can't do this right now.'

And next minute I'm wobbling down the corridor. And when I see Leon I just lose it completely and burst into tears. I won't go into the other gory details because it's all just nuts.

D,

'Grant me the serenity to accept the things I cannot
  change,
 The courage to change the things I can,
 And the wisdom to know the difference.'

Fair enough, but how do you get the courage in the first
place, and how do you know what to change?

Dear Jo,

*I'm really sorry our visit didn't work out the other day. But
it's not the end of the world. And even though we didn't get
to talk I still feel like we made some progress. I just want
you to know, Jo, that I'm always here for you. Whenever
you want to talk I'm ready. Or if you don't want to talk
then that's fine too.*

> *Luv,*
> *Dad*

D,

Even when I go over and over it in my head I still can't figure out what went wrong. I guess I just panicked. But why? Last night Dot came to see me. She sat on the bed holding my hand and I felt like a little girl again. I had a memory flashback to when I'd come off my trike in the driveway (I'd been tearing along real fast and the whole thing tipped me off onto the gravel) and Mum was helping pick the stones out of my knee. I didn't cry that day, either. I am so good at not crying. The trick is to think of something else and to keep on thinking of something else until the tears give up and go away. It hurts your throat but it's way better in the long run.

Except that Dot wouldn't let me think of anything else. 'I think there's something you're not telling us, Jo,' she said, and I've never seen her look so serious. But I didn't answer because I was trying to think of other stuff like *is that a new fly in your web there, Charlotte?*

'It's your dad, isn't it?' she said, refusing to be distracted.

(*Well good for you, Charlotte, aren't you the clever one, and hey, isn't the sky blue today?*)

'Jo!'

'Are they new shoes, Dot? Nice colour.'

'Jo, I want you to listen to me.'

'I am.'

'Look … did your dad hurt you?' She's looking me square in the eye.

(*Bugger off, Dot. I was doing so well…*)

'Jo! This is important.' (She has me by the shoulders now.) 'Jo! Answer me! Did your dad hurt you?!'

At first I didn't understand quite what she was on about. But she mistook my look of confusion for a 'yes'. She formed a conclusion and leapt to it. Then she came at me with both guns blazing.

'I knew it!' she said. 'I damn well knew it.' She was shaking now.

'What?'

Her face was distorted. 'Another bastard arsehole in the world!' she declared.

And suddenly the penny dropped and I knew exactly what she was thinking. But … She had it wrong. She thought Dad hurt me like … like … No, Dot. No!

They're used to that kind of stuff in here. Abuse is why a lot of kids end up in places like this. But that's not what happened. It's not my dad who's the monster, Dot. It's me! Don't you see? It's me!

It took me ages to explain and when I finished I was exhausted. Like I'd gone ten rounds in the boxing ring. But no one can beat you up better than you can yourself – that's what Dot says.

It felt good to tell someone at last. Like bursting a boil, it hurt like hell at the time but when it was over there was relief. And Dot was fantastic. She let me tell the whole story without interrupting. She just sat there nodding and patting my hand and nodding and patting my hand again. 'Oh, you poor wee soul,' she said, which I knew wasn't true. Because I knew deep down that I was not a poor wee soul but it felt good to hear someone say it.

Then Dot said I absolutely have to tell Dad.

I said I'd think about it.

D,

Veronica came by later and we had quite a long talk about eating disorders. I guess, like most of the kids in here, I like to think I'm different. I know I'm definitely not as bad as they are. Even when I'm admitting things in therapy, underneath I'm saying, 'This doesn't apply to me because I'm not as sick as them'. I can't be, can I? My throwing up is under control and my eating is under control – that's what I tell myself. I'm coping. You'll see. Even when I'm put on bed rest I know it's a complete over-reaction on their part. So, it takes a lot to admit it's not. And I'm not quite there yet.

The next time Dad visits he comes straight to my room. I'd been on bed rest for three days and he sat in the chair holding my hand. Nervously biting his lip, he talked about the weather and rugby and Matt's latest creepy crawly. 'God knows how the poor thing survived in that glass jar.' And, 'Did you get the moa tooth, Jo? Strange boy, our Matt — strange boy…' He waffled on trying to fill up the silence and I just lay on the bed with all this stuff building up in my head.

'Dad?'

'Yes, Jo?'

'Dad —'

'Yes, Jo —'

'Well, um, you know when Mum left…?' Fear clogged my throat and I still wasn't sure I could do this.

Dad took my hand. My throat tightened. He looked at me hard and I noticed something I'd never seen before. The pain behind his eyes.

'It's okay, Jo,' he said. 'The nurse already told me —'

Dear old Dot, I thought. And then it started. So unexpectedly, that my normal defence systems were unprepared. One minute I was looking at Dad and swallowing like crazy and the next I was a snivelling wreck. Floods of tears gushed out so fast I couldn't keep up. Heaving and snorting and choking …

Dad didn't say a word, just held my hand and waited. And then I noticed that he was crying too. Not out of control snorting like me, but there were big fat tears rolling down his face. Then he wrapped his arms round me so tight I felt like I was going to break.

And then, just when I felt like it was all going to be okay, he did something unexpected.

He got up and walked out the door.

D,

I have this recurring dream.

In the dream Mum comes to visit but she doesn't recognise me. She's standing in the doorway asking if anyone knows a Johanna Morrison and I yell out 'Mum! It's me!' and rush over but she ignores me and walks off. And then I'm calling after her and she's walking and walking and not turning round once. Pathetic, huh?

I guess seven years is a long time. What if she doesn't recognise me if we meet again? Or, even worse – what if I don't recognise her? For a while after she left I thought about her all the time and I got obsessed about stuff. Like her smell, for instance. I'd go into the bedroom, open the wardrobe door and bury my head in her red winter coat. I told myself that as long as I could smell her she couldn't disappear. But then I panicked and I started worrying that I might be over-sniffing. I might sniff her smell away. So I kept out of the wardrobe so that her smell might last longer.

I haven't been in the wardrobe for ages now.

2:38a.m. is the worst time to be awake. That's when all the dark thoughts surface, hunting you down and dragging you into the gloom. Into those inky depths.

Miss Hughes told me once that if I accepted that Mum was gone for good then maybe I'd be able to get on with things. Move forward, that's how she put it.

'I don't mean to be cruel, dear,' she said, in her counsellor's voice. 'But –'

Exactly. There are still way too many 'buts'. Miss Hughes doesn't know the full story.

'I wish you were dead'. That's what I said. How cruel is that?

Miss Hughes doesn't realise that accepting the fact that Mum might be dead also means accepting that it was me who wished she was in the first place. And I'm not ready to do that. Not yet!

Dear Jo,

As you know I'm not much good with words. In fact I'm pretty useless. The other day when the nurse told me what you'd told her I felt gutted. How could I have been such a jerk not to realise what was happening to you? Well, maybe your Pop was right because I've made a pretty poor job of things so far. Like when I came to visit, for example. I should have known what to say, but I didn't. I had absolutely no idea.

But there is one thing that you have to believe, Jo. And it's this –

Your mother leaving was not your fault. You were nine years old, for goodness' sake. You were NOT responsible. Do you hear me? NOT responsible.

Your mum wasn't well. It wouldn't have mattered what anyone said or didn't say to her. She was severely depressed and not thinking straight. *The doctor said she was suicidal – did I ever tell you that? Well, perhaps I should have!*

The tragic thing was, she wished herself dead. That's the truth of it.

So her leaving had absolutely nothing to do with anything you said to her. Nothing!

Luv, Dad

P.S. You absolutely have to believe that, Jo.

D,

I've had a letter from Dad. Thank God for that. The way he walked out that day really threw me and it took me ages to open his letter. I was so nervous because I thought he must be shocked and disappointed. I thought he must be pretty pissed off as well. And so he should be.

But he sounded okay.

He said it wasn't my fault and that means a lot. I know it's not exactly true but it feels good to hear him say it. (Well, to read him say it.) The thing is, I still feel guilty about Mum and I probably always will. But I'm not going to let it ruin my life – not any more. I wrote a long letter to Dad explaining things but I changed my mind because I know he's not into all that therapy stuff.

So I made it brief and businesslike.

Dear Dad,

Thanks for your letter. I really appreciate it. And I do
believe it, sort of.
    Luv,
    Jo

P.S. Can you and Matt come visit this Saturday?

Dear Jo,

We'll both be there, definitely. See you then.
    Luv,
    Dad

Veronica's favourite saying –
    The longest journey begins with the smallest step.

D,

Tuesday – Muesli, yoghurt, 1 apple, pita bread with chicken. (And I didn't throw up!)

This morning when I got out of the shower I had this bizarre experience. When I looked in the mirror it was like stepping into a horror movie, or one of those kinky mirrors they have at the museum, because looking back at me was a skeleton. Honestly, there were bones all over the place and even my face is full of bones. I spent the afternoon bawling and am still struggling not to throw up in disgust.

Veronica says it's a good sign. She says one of the things about anorexia is that even when you're skin and bone you still think you're fat because your mind starts playing tricks. I still feel as big as a house but I'm working on it – trying to put things in perspective. I still feel petrified about putting on weight, though. The other day, Veronica asked me to try and explain why I felt so frightened and I thought about it for ages. And the answer I came up with is pretty weird.

I told Veronica that I think maybe I'm afraid to 'have' weight because I'm kind of scared to be who I am. I know it sounds dumb, but ... well, if I'm light then I don't have a say or what I say won't really matter. Does that make any sense?

'Are you saying that you don't want a say in your own life, then?' asks Veronica. 'Like, maybe, subconsciously, you don't want to pull your weight in the world?'

Maybe. Yes. Maybe I am frightened of having a say in the world. But after I thought about it some more I knew it wasn't true. Because I do want to have a say in the world. I've always wanted a say, that's been my problem.

'Your daughter certainly has a lot to say for herself,' one of the teachers told Mum and Dad at my first school interview. (Dad told me that.) See, I know that I'm not naturally timid and shy, like Pip, for instance. And I'm not frightened of success, like Ingrid seems to be. Or frightened of who I am, and what the world thinks of me, like Leon. Some of the people in this place don't want a say in the world. I can see that. It's sad.

'Let me be weightless and empty and light...' – that's what Francine wrote. But that's not me. Not really.

Veronica says I have turned the most important corner. It's scary. Sometimes people never get to this corner (like poor Francine, for instance). She says I have a good chance of recovering. And I am determined to get better (I will. I will. I will. I can. I can. I can) – because I absolutely don't want to spend the rest of my life obsessing about what goes in my mouth. I want to be strong and healthy again and to have my say in the world. I really, really do.

So ... here's the plan.

First, I'm going to take things one day at a time and when I get to 49 kilos I'll be allowed home. (I know it was supposed to be 50 kilos but I managed to negotiate!) Then, when I'm home, I'll come back to hospital once a week as a day patient. I'll have a counselling session with Veronica and get weighed weekly. So far I've managed to put on two kilos. Who would have thought putting on weight would be so scary??!!

Wednesday – I had a swim today and it was totally utterly awesome.

Dear Issy,

Guess what?! I am now officially 48 kilos, which means
I have just one kilo to go before I am allowed home. That
is great but also very scary news because the weird thing
about being in hospital is that the longer you stay in here
the more it seems like home and the more home seems like
somewhere else. Dot says it's called being institutionalised.

I guess you get used to the routine and to not thinking for yourself. And maybe you feel safe. It's kind of like
weird becomes normal and normal becomes weird. I know
that going back to school will be pretty scary after being
in hospital. And it's amazing when I look back to when
I first arrived and thought I'd come to prison. I was such a
tosser. Sometimes I can't believe how angry I was. Going
through your letters to me feels so weird, realising how
I must have seemed to you.

I am sooo looking forward to seeing you again, Issy –
your letters have been like a lifeline to me and God knows
how I'd have got through all this stuff without you.
Don't let that go to your head, though. It doesn't mean
I'm going to let you thump me at tennis or anything.

Actually, I'm a bit worried about getting together for
real again. Are you?

Anyway, I just wanted to warn you that I'll be home
again soon.

Luv,

Jo

Dear Jo,

I can't wait for you to come back to school. You don't know how relieved I am. I was worried out of my wits and when that Francine girl died … well, it didn't bear thinking about, Jo.

Luv,

Issy

P.S. I'll book the tennis court for Friday afternoon.
P.P.S. 'Failing to plan is like planning to fail.' Miss Haddock has just put that on the whiteboard, which means you will be back just in time for exams. Good timing, Jo.

D,

Friday – one plate ice cream, two spoonfuls tinned apricots, half a cup of runner beans, one sausage, one plate of pasta!! (Not thrown up!)

Yahoo … today I'm going home!!!

Dear Dot,

It's hard to believe it's been a whole month. In some
ways it feels like no time has passed at all and, in other
ways, it's like I've been home again forever. I won't say
it's been easy. It hasn't! In fact, when I first came home
I was totally miserable and all I wanted to do was slink
back into hospital, crawl under the sheets and hide. I felt
hopeless and it felt weird with Dad and Matt being super
nice to me all the time. To be honest they drove me crazy
– like I was some china doll. I felt like they were watching
everything I did and I know for sure they were watching
everything I ate. It was like being under surveillance 24/7,
which was worse than when I first went into hospital. The
first few weeks were hideous.

Since then I've had some good days and bad days. I
still have to write down everything I eat, which gets fairly
tedious at times. And I can't say I have completely stopped
throwing up or that I am back to normal with my eating.
If I'm under stress there's always the temptation and I
wonder if I'm ever going to be normal again.

Actually, I'm starting to wonder if there even is such
a thing as normal. Everywhere you go these days people
are doing some kind of diet or other and once you start
thinking a lot about food it's very hard to go back to not
thinking much about it. (After all, it's not something you
can actually give up, like cigarettes or something. Instead
you have to totally relearn how to eat.) But I hope I am

not as obsessed and strange about food as I was.

School was difficult at first. I was so behind with everything and it felt pretty scary going back, kind of like I was the new girl or something. Everyone acted strange with me at the start. Also, I got back just in time for the practice NCEA exams, which was bad timing and I managed to fail pretty much everything except for English. (I think I have Miss Haddock to thank for that.)

And thank God for Issy who has been utterly fantastic. She even got me a place on the school newspaper, which I am still reserving judgement about. Don't laugh, Dot but I write this fake Agony Aunt column. Pretty sad, huh?! Stuff like *Dear Aunty Jo, I am thinking about getting green dreadlocks but know my mum will go psycho, what do you think*? If I get stuck for an answer I find staring into space for an hour or two quite helpful, especially when it's a starry night.

Mostly I'm just trying to get by one day at a time. I guess you might have heard I still see Veronica once a week as an outpatient and Miss Hughes keeps an eye on me as well. Miss Hughes is actually not so bad when you get to know her, like the other day I told her about the letters I'd written Mum when I was in hospital. I was worried she might think I was unhinged or something but she took it in her stride. Amazingly, she didn't laugh hysterically and get the straitjacket out (which I'm sure she keeps in her file cabinet for emergencies!). She even said she thought it might be helpful for my recovery. I tell her how I feel now – well, a little. (Still find it hard to do the touchy feely thing.)

Say hi to everyone for me, won't you? Have you heard how Leon's doing? I seem to have lost his address.

I hope all is going well for you, Dot.

Luv,

Jo

P.S. Would you mind looking in on Charlotte from time to time – just to make sure the cleaning lady doesn't suck her down the vacuum cleaner?

P.P.S. My friend Issy is now officially going out with Tim from Year Twelve. And she wants to hook me up with some friend of his called Larry… I'm still undecided.

P.P.S. I would be really grateful if you could get me Leon's address.

Dear Jo,

Hi. It's me, Dot. How nice to get your letter. I'm
so pleased to hear you are doing okay. You are one
of my favourite patients and I knew as soon as you
arrived that you were going to make it. Some don't,
you know. Some come back here time and time again.
It's very sad and I don't know what the answer is.
But you are going to be fine and that's the main
thing.

I don't think I'm supposed to get addresses (it's
all to do with the privacy act) but I can't see the
harm in it and what they don't know won't hurt
them.

Keep well and out of trouble.
Lots of love,
Dot

P.S. Good luck with your column.
P.P.S. Give Leon my best wishes when you make contact.

Dear Leon,

I've wanted to write for ages but getting hold of your
address was no mean feat. It's all this privacy act stuff.
Seems like it's okay to know about someone's personal
hang-ups but not their home address and telephone number.
Thank God for Dot who has become a very talented
sleuth since her husband did the dirty. I didn't ask how
she did it but I have visions of her sneaking into Plaquey's
office under cover of darkness with a dodgy torch and a
pair of surgical gloves to eliminate fingerprints.

I've been thinking about you lots, Leon. Mainly because
I've just found the pile of Trivial Pursuit cards I had
stashed in my suitcase. Okay – confession time …

Yes, I did have cheating on my mind. My plan was to
memorise them systematically and then wow you with my
brilliance. Doesn't seem quite so important now. Funny
the things you get obsessed by – or distracted with. Guess
it served a purpose though, aye. Those games we had
together probably saved my sanity.

Speaking of sanity – how's yours? I hope that guitar
stuff wasn't just a distraction because you were getting
really good and music is such a healing thing and should
definitely help with getting your shit together. You're
lucky in that respect. Did I tell you I was completely
tone deaf? Honestly, I'm so bad at singing that our music
teacher once asked if I'd mind just mouthing the words
because I was putting the others off, which certainly put

a dampener on my rock star aspirations.

Anyway, I hope you're still strumming away and making up the odd song or two.

You'll be pleased to know I'm finally making progress with getting my own shit together. Sometimes it feels like two steps forward and three back but at least I'm moving forward. Enough about me, though.

I'd really like to know how *you're* getting on and if you feel like dropping me a line, Leon, I'd love to hear from you.

Keep strumming,

Luv,

Jo

Dear Jo,

Good old Dot, eh.

Sorry it's taken me so long to get back to you but my home address has changed so your letter took a few detours. The thing is, I'm living with Gran now. Long story but you won't be surprised to hear that the 'happy families' thing didn't work out. To be honest it was even crappier than I thought it would be.

In the end I figured I had two choices.

Tell them I'm gay and go or tell them I'm gay and stay. So I took the coward's way out and left them to it. I decided it was their problem, not mine. Actually, that was Gran's idea. 'If they're not grown-up enough to accept you for who you are then they don't deserve you,' she said. 'You can come live with me instead.'

So I'm now living in a one-bedroom pensioner's flat by the beach, which isn't near as bad as it sounds. The wrinklies are a real hoot and old Mrs Reynolds next door has taught me to body board. It's great. We waddle down to the surf at six every morning except for Sunday because that's her day for salsa dancing and she needs to save her energy.

The people round here aren't scared to have fun and they've been round long enough to know what's important in life. Well, that's what Gran says.

Gran is really on my case these days, which is good because self-motivation was never my strong point. Next term she's got me signed up for a barista's course at the polytech. Don't worry, I'm not going to be a lawyer or anything daft but I will learn how to make great cappuccino. Maybe you and Issy can be my guinea pigs. You are welcome to visit any time,

Jo. I'll even set up the Trivial Pursuit if you like. Keep in touch.

Leon.

Dear Mum,

You'll be pleased to know that I have finally been released from the Camp for the Gifted and Talented. It was an interesting experience but one I don't want to repeat in the near future. Gifted and talented is very hard work and I would happily settle for ordinary and boring just now. In fact, I think ordinary and boring is very underrated.

Everyone is fine at home and school is pretty much the same way I left it.

Except for something weird that happened today that I want to tell you about. We were in the library for last period and there was a display of animal fiction books down by where the computers are. And they had loads of different titles like *Tiger Rising*, *Lionboy*, *Moby Dick*, *Black Beauty*, *Stuart Little* (I've read them all, by the way) and *Charlotte's Web*.

When I saw *Charlotte's Web* I got goose bumps because I hadn't seen that book in years and the cover looked so familiar and everything. I actually went giddy because I knew that there were two chapters I needed to read.

Remember how we never finished it because we thought it was going to be too sad? Well, I thought I might be up to it now, so I sat down to read.

I got all the way to the page that said 'Charlotte is very ill. She has only a short time to live' and I almost chickened out. But I carried on and guess what? You should read it because the ending wasn't quite as sad as we thought. Of course, Charlotte dies, like we knew she would, but good things happen as well. Like Templeton (the rat) does this amazing rescue and gets her egg sac (with five hundred and fourteen! unborn children) back to the barn.

In the springtime the eggs hatch and although most of the newborn spiders set off to make their own way in the world three of them stay behind, in the barn. Their names are Joy, Aranea and Nellie. And because Wilbur owes his life to Charlotte, he pledges his friendship to her daughters forever. It's so sweet, Mum. Such a sweet, lovely story. You'd enjoy it. I know you would.

At the end it has a line that says: 'It is not often that someone comes along who is a true friend and a good writer.'

Yeah, I thought. And I know someone exactly like that.

A Teachers' Resource Kit for

Losing it

is available from
www.longacre.co.nz

Check out our website for more
Longacre Press Young Adult titles.